DARING

KYLIE GILMORE

Daring: © 2022 by Kylie Gilmore

Cover design by: Michele Catalano Creative

Published by: Extra Fancy Books

ISBN-13: 978-1-64658-033-0

The world needs positive people!

1

Skylar

The first time I met Gage Williams, I didn't like him very much. And let me just say, I usually like everyone. First thing he did when we met was shoot down my interior design idea while I was pitching to new potential clients for work on an inn. And he called me Miss Perky. The world needs positive people, Mr. Grumps!

Despite that rocky start, the second time we met, I managed to make it through an entire inn renovation with him by drawing on Herculean reserves of patience. The clients were so happy with the results, they brought us both back to work on the inn's new restaurant. And get this: when I tried to review the design plans with Gage at the ground breaking, instead of a *normal* back-and-forth conversation, he rattled off the building specs and then said, "Now get out of my way." Seriously! I've got no time for an alpha male with a 'tude.

Deep breath.

I had a two-month break from Mr. Grumps while the restaurant was being constructed, and now I'm back for design work. This is the prime time for design tweaks before construction on the interior is complete. I'm determined on this third try at a work relationship to be the bigger person and not let him tweak my temper. I am the consummate professional at all costs.

Gage approaches, tool belt hanging low on his narrow hips, as he talks to a guy on crew. "I should get someone to stage my house before I put it on the market."

My ears perk up. That sounds like a job for an interior designer.

"I've seen your place," the guy says. "It's like an empty white box."

Gage grumbles something about flipping houses, and then gives him instructions for dealing with an electrician. The crew guy walks to the back of the space.

I square my shoulders and straighten my spine. I could stage Gage's house to sell. My mind immediately flashes to designing for his tastes. He'd probably like steel and glass for the interior with barbed wire around the perimeter of the property. Ha!

"Gage, if you have a minute," I say when he reaches me.

"Nope."

He strides so quickly toward the front door to get some supply or another I'd have to sprint to catch up with him. It's a freezing cold December morning in Summerdale, New York. Not happening in my vintage lavender moccasins with lime green tassels. I'd have to change back into boots for the snowy front yard. I'm tempted to throw a moccasin at the back of his head, but then he's gone. And I'm a pacifist! I swear he purposely makes himself unavailable to me. We have to work together as a team.

Grrr...

Staging his house is out. I don't care how desperately I need work. I could never have him as a client, even if I am currently home displaced. The condo I used to rent was sold, so I had to move out, which is just as well because I couldn't afford the rent anymore due to reasons I try not to dwell on. I'm currently crashing at my brother's place.

Not that Gage would ever ask me to work for him in a million years, which is fine by me. No paycheck would be worth the aggravation.

After this job, I'll be working on the renovation of my client's house next door (also with Gage, unfortunately), and then I've got a whole lot of nothing on the horizon. The reason for my epic fail as a solo interior designer is a shameful secret that follows me around like a dark cloud overhead.

And there's no going back to my old design firm. That door has been closed forever.

Well, at least Gage is so irritating it's easy to keep a professional distance. I learned the hard way to dim my naturally sunny disposition at work in favor of a mask of professionalism. Part of me says I shouldn't change for anyone, but I can't risk getting burned again. I have to be very careful never to send mixed signals at work, especially to men.

I walk over to Gage, where he's now directing some guys hauling in sinks for the restroom. He's in his late twenties and founded his own construction company at eighteen. Talk about fearless. I'll give him that. As usual, his expression is stone. I should probably call him Mr. Stonewall instead of Mr. Grumps since that's what he mostly does—stonewall me. His short dark brown hair is shaved on the sides, emphasizing his sharp cheekbones.

My eyes are involuntarily drawn to his forearms—an incredibly masculine combo of muscle, tendons, and raised blood vessels covered in ink. His left forearm sports a geometric-shaped outline of a deer tattoo and a compass is on the other. I often find myself studying his tattoos. Only because they're interesting. I do *not* have a thing for muscular inked forearms. Really.

I give him my polite professional smile. "Good morning."

Gage gives me the briefest of glances. Not even the scruff on his jaw can soften that stone-cold expression. "What?"

I bristle. See what I mean? Man with a 'tude. I bite back a lesson on basic manners and move smoothly to the issue at hand. "A ventless gas fireplace for the reception area. No chimney necessary."

"No."

"Spencer agreed." That's our client.

"No." Gage is a man of few words and even fewer explanations. It drives me batty.

"It's good ambiance, and it keeps the reception area from getting drafty while people are waiting for a table."

"That's what the bar is for. Let them get cold and move to the bar for a whiskey to warm up."

At least we've moved beyond "no."

"Not everyone wants a drink to warm up. What if it's a pregnant woman or even a child or just someone who doesn't drink?"

His expression remains stone. "I've got a lot of things on my plate. This isn't one of them."

And then he walks away.

I fume for a moment before following him, determined to reason with the unreasonable man. "If it helps, I can have the fireplace company send someone to install it, so it won't affect your schedule in the least." That's his mantra—on time and on budget.

"It doesn't."

"Why not?"

He barks out some orders to the crew working in the restroom. Then he turns and nearly walks into me, his brows lifting. "You're still here?"

I press my lips in a flat line in an attempt to keep from snapping at him. It wouldn't be professional to call him a rigid bosshole, now would it? Not that he's my boss. Spencer and Paige are my clients for this project, and Spencer agreed with my fireplace idea. "It won't take time from your crew if I bring an installer in from the fireplace company. Spencer will cover the cost."

"Then there's permits and inspections. Schedule busted." He strides to the back of the space, where he starts setting up sawhorses for his next project.

I follow him, of course. Spencer wants this, and now's the time to implement it. Gage stares at my moccasins.

"What?" I ask.

His brows scrunch together. "Where did you find those shoes?"

"A cool thrift shop. They're vintage and very comfortable." I've always been a fan of thrift shops with their interesting pieces.

"Uh-huh."

I exhale sharply. "Look, Paige and Spencer want me to have input while things are still under construction. It's much easier to make changes now than when it's done. There's always some wiggle room." *With reasonable people anyway.*

He gives me a deadpan look. "I don't wiggle."

I'd laugh if I weren't so exasperated with his rigid stance on sticking to the plan. The best ideas happen organically as things unfold. Plans can change.

"Stand back," he orders and pulls a large sheet of wood paneling across the sawhorses.

I take a deep calming breath. This is not the first tweak he's turned down. More like the millionth! What am I doing here if I can't do my job properly? Aargh!

Breathe. I will persist nevertheless, as women must to achieve their goals. "Gage."

He puts his goggles on and gets the saw into position.

I swear if he starts that saw while I'm talking . . .

I force a pleasant expression. "If I can find a time savings for your plan somewhere, then would you be open to the idea of working a fireplace into the reception area?"

"No."

I narrow my eyes. "Not an acceptable answer. I need an explanation or some flexibility here. Use your words, Mr. Grumps." *Oops.* I usually only use that name in my private rantings, but he's really, really irritating and preventing me from doing my job to the best of my abilities.

A trace of amusement lights his brown eyes, which makes me more incensed. He thinks it's funny when I get mad at him. Before Gage, I never fought with anyone. Never *once* lost my temper. I'm a kind, loving person who only wants to put good into the world.

"Well, Miss Perky," he drawls, "you stick to your plan, and I'll stick to mine."

I hate when he calls me Miss Perky. I'm not that naively

friendly woman anymore. I'm a coolheaded professional, dammit!

"It's just a tweak to the plan," I say in an even tone. No temper here. No perkiness either.

No response from Gage. His expression is hard, his jaw set.

I know the real power player in this scenario, and I'm not afraid to use her. "Then I'm going over your head to Paige—"

RR-RR-RR. The circular saw drowns me out as he gets back to work.

Note to self: add him to the small list of people I'd like to throw into a volcano.

I turn on my heel. This isn't over.

2

"Skylar Bellamy, what happened to you?"

I jackknife upright in my seat as though I've been caught doodling in my notebook in class instead of paying attention. Funny how hearing your strict third-grade teacher's voice again can bring you back to misbehaving student so quickly. Mrs. Joan Ellis or—as some people call her behind her back for her stern, strict nature—General Joan regularly smacked her ruler on my desk to get my attention. She just walked into the meeting room at the Summerdale library, took one look at me, and sized up my current predicament—flailing.

And not a *Kermit the frog gleeful* flail. More like a *fish caught on dry land* flail.

I flash my pearly whites. "Hi, Mrs. Ellis, long time no see. Thought I'd help out with the Winterfest committee since I'm back in town for a job."

Mrs. Ellis sits with a quiet *oomph* next to me and studies me with her sharp brown eyes. I'm guessing she's late eighties by now, maybe even ninety, with short white hair parted to the side in a cute wave. She dresses nice with a red scarf tied around her neck, a button-down white blouse, and gray trousers. She's been a widow for as long as I've known her.

I twirl a lock of my long dark brown hair automatically, a

self-soothing gesture since childhood, and glance across the table at Nicholas, owner of a small grocery store in town, who's looked like Santa for as long as I can remember. The other members of the committee aren't here yet. See, this is why it doesn't pay to be early. I just couldn't stand another moment alone at my place. When I'm alone, the doubts creep in. I have to remain positive or my current flail will turn into an irreversible flop. Career over; prospects zero.

"You look terrible," Mrs. Ellis says, getting right to the point. "You're much too young to have bags under your eyes. And your skin is sallow. Go home right now and get some sleep."

"It's not even seven yet," I protest. Then I remember she's not my teacher anymore, and I'm a twenty-six-year-old grown-ass woman.

I stifle a sigh. Sometimes I'm so tired of adulting. I wish I could go back to that innocent childhood time when I was happy at my lakeside home, painting a fairyland mural on my bedroom wall, hunting for fairies around the lake with my older brothers, splashing together in the water. Now it's all anxiety all the time, trying to build my solo interior design business before I run out of funds and have to admit to my brothers that once again I leaped before I looked and FAILED. The money from the sale of our childhood home —gone.

My older brothers adore me. I'm the free spirit no one in my family takes seriously. At this point in my life, I want to prove I can make it on my own. I don't need anyone to rescue me because I know what I'm doing. I'm just having a rough patch.

I straighten my spine and pull my shoulders back. "I'll sleep after the meeting." I smile at General Joan. Sorry, it's tough not to see her as a general when you're the one she's focused her laser-beam eyes on. "You're looking well."

"I take care of myself," General Joan replies tartly with a pointed look that indicates I'm failing at it. "What's wrong?"

I try for a pleasant expression. "Nothing."

"I heard you're working over at the inn."

"I was. Now I'm doing the interior design work for the restaurant next door."

"I always thought you'd become an artist."

I press my lips together. Mom encouraged my creativity, but always urged me to choose a practical career. I understood why. Dad left when I was four and never paid child support, so money was tight. Interior design lets me pay the bills while turning people's homes into a work of art. Kinda. I still have to follow the client's taste, which isn't always mine. And paying the bills? Even crashing at my brother Max's place, I still have to eat, oh, and pay off my giant student loans. A temporary situation, I assure myself. I'm not mooching off my brother forever, especially when he'll start asking questions. Something has to pan out. Otherwise, I'll have to admit to Max that I need help and why. I don't want anyone to know my secret, especially not my big brother, who'll make a big deal and then take over in typical rescue mode. I can handle this myself.

"I grew up," I finally say in answer to her subtle poke at why I'm not an artist.

"You were quite gifted," she says, rubbing it in.

"Thank you."

"Your art still hangs in Town Hall."

I incline my head. That was my senior year project in high school—a painting of Lake Summerdale in the fall, the trees in their vibrant foliage of red, orange, and yellow reflected in the water like soft candle flames. It was my view for my entire childhood living on the lake.

"Do you have love in your life?" General Joan asks out of nowhere.

I blink, shocked to hear the stern teacher talking about love. "Uh, are you asking if I have a boyfriend?"

Her eyes bore into mine, waiting for my answer.

"Not at the moment."

"Recent breakup?"

I shift uneasily. "No. I just haven't found anyone to get serious about in a while." I don't know how to explain to General Joan that guys in my generation aren't what you'd

call real big on commitment. I've only had one serious relationship, four years ago in college. We broke up when he
moved to Michigan for graduate school. Now he's a philos-
ophy professor out there. I wish him well.

"Is that the problem?" she asks.

"I don't have a problem."

Nicholas, aka Summerdale Santa, chuckles. "Joan, leave
her be. She's here to help, not be interrogated."

Her head whips toward him. "And I'm helping her." She
turns to me. "Max tells me you're doing well, going out on
your own, and working on multiple projects in town. If it's
not a professional problem, it must be personal."

"It *is* personal." *As in, I don't want to share.*

"I knew it!" She pats my arm. "Don't give it another
thought. I'm quite good at this."

"Good at what?"

Nicholas laughs. *Ho-ho.* I swear he works at being Santa.
He's even wearing red suspenders over his white cotton shirt
that hugs a pot belly. To be fair, it's a week and a half until
Christmas. Maybe he's just getting into the spirit of things.

The other members of the committee file in—mostly
people around thirty from Max's grade in school. I wonder if
they were waiting to walk in at the last minute to avoid an
interrogation from General Joan. Note to self: find out where
the rest of the committee hides out before the meeting.

Audrey, the librarian, takes her seat and smiles at me. She
looks like you might expect a librarian to look, her dark hair
in a messy bun and her blouse with a Peter Pan collar
buttoned all the way to the top. She and my brother Max
were madly in love in high school. I always liked her, super
sweet and kind. Her friends join her.

Surprisingly, Drew Robinson walks in and takes a seat at
the end of the table. I say surprisingly because my memory
of Drew is more of a lone wolf. He runs a karate dojo and
used to be an Army Ranger, which is an elite unit of
soldiers. To say he's intimidating with his glower and ultra-
buff stature would be an understatement. His dark brown
hair is on the longish side, his jaw square, his eyes sharp

and alert. Even in a black thermal Henley and jeans, he looks like a would-be assassin. And he's going to help plan Winterfest with hot chocolate by the lake, kiddy games, ice skating, and the crowning of the royal court's King Frost and Queen Snowflake? Something doesn't add up here. Has Winterfest become a covert operation for some security issue in town?

I gasp at the sharp jab in the ribs from General Joan. "Ouch! I'm paying attention." I scowl because everyone's still talking casually. "The meeting hasn't even started yet."

She leans close to whisper in my ear, "That one is spoken for. I saw you eying Drew. I've got someone else in mind for you."

"I'm perfectly fine being single," I say through my teeth.

"And I'm perfectly happy to help. I've helped dozens of people find love right here in town." Wow, General Joan gives herself a lot of credit. Does she really think she was the reason people fell in love? When I was in love, I walked around in a daze of light, floaty happiness. I can't imagine General Joan in that picture at all.

I quirk my lips to the side, refraining from comment.

She pats her short white hair. "It's nice to pick up a hobby in retirement. Just call me Cupid."

I nearly choke on a laugh because the last thing I'd call the stern-looking general is Cupid, but then I realize she's dead serious. A chill runs down my spine. I do *not* want senior-citizen matchmaking on top of all my other problems. I look around, desperately hoping someone will call the meeting to order, but everyone's laughing and talking like the old friends they are, except Drew, who's silently surveying the room in a way that says he's on guard. Against what I'm not sure. We're in a glass-enclosed meeting room in the second-story loft of the library. No enemies hiding here.

"I'm going to find you a fellow," General Joan says to me.

Except maybe the enemy in plain sight next to me.

She gestures to Mayor Levi across the table from us and definitely within hearing distance. "A good one like Levi here."

Omigod. I've never been set up in my life, let alone by an elderly Cupid in front of the guy.

Levi turns at his name, smiling. He's thirtyish and handsome with his dark hair and beard, but I'm not looking for a setup. These things need to happen organically. "What's that about me?"

General Joan gives him a hard look. "Are you getting enough to eat in your lonely bachelor house?"

He stops smiling and says in a tired voice, "Yes, Mrs. Ellis. Thank you for asking." *Probably not the first time she's asked.* He looks around the room. "Should we get started?"

"Yes," General Joan says, slapping the table for emphasis. "First order of business. Skylar has a problem."

Kill me now.

I hold up a palm. "It's nothing. Really. So where are we with Winterfest this year? Still planning on bringing back the royal court and ball? I'd love to help with that."

"Her problem is a lack of love in her life," General Joan announces.

I stiffen, my gaze locked on Levi, dreading what she'll say next. Except Levi is casually reviewing his notes. I risk a look around the room. Drew is staring at Audrey, Audrey's cringing on my behalf, and everyone else is busting a gut trying not to laugh.

"Levi—" General Joan starts.

I cut her off before she can force him to ask me out in front of everyone. "The real problem is Gage, the contractor I'm forced to put up with for all of my Summerdale projects."

She wants a problem to fix? Let her fix Gage. Not my career-killing secret or my lack of a love life. I warm to my chosen target because he's got all the makings of someone who needs General Joan on his case. He's closed off, harsh, and never shakes things up. Always focused with his tunnel vision, missing the bigger picture due to one of his major flaws—zero flexibility. Well, guess what? That kind of narrowminded focus is how you miss all the best things in life. Once General Joan gets through with him, he'll *have* to be nicer to me. Maybe then we can finally have a productive working relationship.

"I look forward to meeting this Gage fellow," General Joan says. "I'll straighten him out."

See?

I smile, feeling lighter already. Her focus is off me, and maybe this'll make Gage easier to work with. "Just don't mention my name to him."

"Of course," she says with a sly look that immediately sets every nerve in my body on high alert.

Uh-oh. Did I just make things worse for myself on my only job for the foreseeable future?

3

Gage

I look down at the petite elderly woman glaring at me on my worksite. "Who are you again?"

Who let her in?

Her brown eyes are sharp and boring through my brain with some kind of X-ray vision to read my soul.

She thrusts out her hand, and I give it a quick shake. "Joan Ellis. I'm from the Summerdale welcoming committee. I need to know your birthday. It's a thing we do."

I run a hand through my short hair. I really don't have time for this. "It's not safe for you to be here, ma'am. This is a construction zone." I gesture around me, though it's obvious. Wires hanging from the ceiling, a crew guy sawing away, another one using a nail gun to put in the new windows.

She looks around. "The restaurant is shaping up. Are you on schedule?"

"Always."

A guy on crew comes up to me. "Having an issue with the placement of the bathroom sconces over the sinks."

"Be there in a minute."

Another guy calls to me from across the room, asking for the go-ahead on some sheetrock by the coat closet. I gesture for him to go on and pull my phone out, noting items done.

"Are you the boss?"

I refocus on the woman in front of me, who doesn't seem inclined to leave. "Yup. My company, says so on the T-shirt." I gesture to the guys with Williams Construction and Remodeling on the backs of their shirts. I'm wearing one too under my flannel shirt.

"How long have you owned the company? And, more importantly, is it doing well?"

I glance around. "Are you a reporter?"

Her lips purse disapprovingly, reminding me of my fifth-grade teacher, a woman completely over being a teacher and not happy with any of us. "I told you I'm from the Summerdale welcoming committee. I'm trying to get to know our newest resident."

"I'm not a resident. I commute from New Jersey."

"How's Williams Construction and Remodeling doing?"

It occurs to me that maybe she wants some work done on her house, so I switch into sales mode. "Very well, thanks. Been in business for nine years with many happy clients." I pull my wallet from my back pocket, fish out a business card, and hand it over. "Everything you need to know is there on my website. Now I really need to get back to work. We have a lot to do before the holidays."

"Birthday?"

I let out a breath of exasperation. "January twelfth."

"How old will you be? We need to have the candle count right."

I look around, wondering if anyone else noticed this strange old woman trespassing on a work site. The crew's working industriously as usual and not paying any attention to us.

"Well?" she demands.

I don't know why she cares, but I figure it's quicker to answer than argue with her. "I'll be twenty-eight."

"Good age for settling down," she says in a voice that brooks no argument.

Weird.

"Ma'am, if you'll excuse me—"

She nods once. "You seem like a focused young man. Got your head on straight. That's good."

I slowly back away. "Nice to meet you, ma'am. Careful on your way out."

"Nice manners too. I like that. Ever have a criminal record?"

I stare at her, bewildered from the jump in logic from manners to crime. "No."

"Any siblings?"

I approach her again, wary. "Why're you asking me so many personal questions?"

"Just trying to get to know the newest member of our community."

"I work here. I live elsewhere." *As I said.*

"That can change. Brothers or sisters?"

I hang my head. This woman just won't leave me alone. I lift my head and give her my sternest stare. "Look, I appreciate the small-town hospitality, but I'm here to do a job."

She bares her teeth in a semblance of a smile. "You have a big-brother vibe about you. Younger sister or brother? How many?"

I shove a hand through my hair. "Just one. Younger sister."

"And what does she do?"

I find myself smiling, thinking about Livvie with her big heart. "She's studying to be a nurse."

"You're proud of her."

"Of course. It's not an easy job, but it suits her." She's graduating with honors this spring. I helped her apply to colleges and get a scholarship. I live only a half hour from her school, and even after I flip my house for my next project, I'll still stay near Livvie. She knows she always has a home with me.

"You work in chaos."

"Oh no. I avoid chaos at all costs. This is all very organized down to the last nail." *Thanks, Mom and Dad, for that chaotic, hellish childhood.* My parents' assets were seized, and Dad went to jail for shady business dealings. Some kids might've fallen apart to go from wealthy to poor the way we did. Me, I straightened up fast, realizing I had nobody to depend on but myself. I looked after Livvie too since Mom could barely hold herself together let alone take care of us.

"I keep my business running smoothly," I add just in case she wants to hire me. "Trust me on that."

She nods in approval, and I stand taller. Wait, why do I care what this woman thinks? I just met her. There's something about her that feels authoritative, like her approval has to be earned.

A feminine voice calls out behind me, "Oh, hi! What a surprise!"

I turn toward Skylar, her wide blue eyes doing something weird to my insides. A tension low in my belly, all my senses on alert. Her long, wavy, dark hair is down, adding to the carefree bohemian look of her outfit—a flowing white and silver polka-dotted blouse with tight black pants and ankle boots. Now there's chaos personified. Skylar's always trying to order me around, changing construction plans to suit her interior design needs. I shut that down right quick. Yet she keeps trying. Persistent as hell.

"Is this your grandmother?" I ask her.

"No." She rushes over to Mrs. Ellis. "Hi! What're you doing here? Have you, uh, been here long?"

Mrs. Ellis gives her a significant look. "I'm with the Summerdale welcoming committee. Just had to add Gage's birthday to the official list."

"Welcoming committee? Oh, well, I'll walk you out." Skylar sends me an apologetic look, though I'm not sure why.

"I had to meet the contractor who's giving you so many problems," Mrs. Ellis whispers loudly. "Don't worry. I didn't mention your name."

Skylar lets out a loud laugh. "Ha-ha-ha, you're so funny! Let me walk you to your car."

I shake my head and walk back toward the saw, where I was working on trimming some wood paneling.

"I can see why you don't like him," Mrs. Ellis announces.

I halt in place by my saw, my back to them but my ears tuned in.

"Can you lower your voice a bit?" Skylar asks.

"What?" Mrs. Ellis says loudly like she's hard of hearing. Though she didn't seem to have any problem hearing me with all the background construction noise.

"Never mind," Skylar says.

Mrs. Ellis shares this next bit loud enough for the whole crew to hear, even with the buzzsaw going. "He's a stick-in-the-mud. Rigid and too serious."

I slowly turn and meet the older woman's eyes. She looks pleased with herself. I'm tempted to tell her what I think about nosey women who disturb a busy workplace, but then Skylar pipes up.

"You see what I have to put up with? And don't get me started on his inflexibility where it concerns design, even when that design is perfectly functional." She nods once in my direction.

I suddenly notice it's quiet. The guys are listening in. "Get back to work," I growl. "We're on a schedule."

Work commences at once, and I return to work too.

A few minutes later, I glance over toward the front door, feeling someone's eyes on me. Skylar's standing there alone, staring at me and wringing her hands together in front of her.

Something's bothering her. Go help.

No, don't engage. You've wasted enough time today.

I fight the impulse to help for a moment longer before crossing the space to her. The woman's in distress, and I can't ignore it.

I play it cool, easing into the conversation. "Don't tell me you want another change in the bar area."

"Yes, but I need to tell you something about Mrs. Ellis."

I blow out a breath. "Make it fast."

She huffs. "I'm busy too, you know. That doesn't mean we can't talk for a few minutes."

I incline my head, waiting to hear what's bothering her. It's tough to wait because I've only got one week left before we shut down for the holidays, and I'd like to get a few things finished up before we go.

She sighs. "Look, I just wanted to say don't mind whatever Mrs. Ellis said to you. I only told her you were a problem so she'd stop trying to set me up with the mayor."

"I'm a problem?"

"Obviously. You shut down every idea I have."

"Only when they cut into my budget or schedule."

Her eyes flash, and that weird feeling in my insides happens again. "Which is every time!"

Even though my work is waiting, I can't help but tease her a little. "You get set up often by the welcoming committee?"

She crosses her arms. "No, well, I guess. I don't know. I don't need a setup. And she just needs a focus."

"I have a focus. Work." I walk back to the saw. If her biggest distress is an old woman trying to set her up, she's fine.

Skylar follows me and grabs my sleeve before I can get the tool running. I stare at her hand on my arm, the first time she's touched me since we started working closely together several months ago. She smooths out the fabric, sort of petting my bicep in the process. Heat rushes through me, and I'm suddenly aware of her in a primal way that makes me feel alive. She smells like warm spice.

Nope, not going there. Never get involved with someone you work with. I learned my lesson with Kate, a former client. Three months into our relationship, she ended it and made the last month of work on her house absolute hell. The worst part was when she informed me I was so closed off that she had to go to therapy because of me. That hit me where it hurts after Mom's stint in a mental hospital. It's better if I just keep to myself with the occasional casual hookup. Outside of work, that is.

"Was Mrs. Ellis harsh with you?" Skylar asks earnestly. "She used to be my third-grade teacher, and we were all scared of her."

"You afraid my feelings got hurt, Miss Perky?"

Her brows crease in the middle. "She did call you a stick-in-the-mud. Rigid and too serious. And I'd add that your narrowminded focus makes you miss all the best things in life."

"Oh, yeah, like what? Sunshine and rainbows?"

She bristles. "Among other things."

"You keep those. I'm doing just fine like I am." I gesture for her to back up a step.

She shifts away, but keeps talking. "Back to the bar thing, I found a gorgeous antique mirror—"

I run the saw, drowning out her request, which I already know won't fit into the plan for the bar.

A few moments later, she slaps a Post-it note on the end of the panel I'm working on and walks away. I lean toward it to read the looping scrawl.

Does not work well with others. Flaw #734.

I burst out laughing and look around for her. Damn, she left. Can't wait to see what else she sees as my flaws. For someone who considers me a problem, she sure pays close attention to me. No one's ever taken the time to catalogue that many flaws of mine. I don't hate it.

Skylar

I weave a gold ribbon in with the greenery on the fireplace mantel and stand back to admire the view. This is the first wedding I've ever been hired to design. On the one hand, it's been an easy project because it's Paige and Spencer's Christmas Eve wedding at the Inn at Lovers' Lane. I know my clients well, and I helped design the inn. On the other hand, I'm feeling the pressure. A reporter and photographer from the national magazine *Bride Special* will be here to feature their wedding and the inn. Everything has to be perfect.

I do a slow turn in the wedding space, soaking it in. I had

the dining room furniture taken out, so it's one large open space between the living room and dining area. Greenery with gold ribbon runs along the fireplace mantel and drapes along the ceiling. Fairy lights run the perimeter of the ceiling, bringing out the shine of the gold ribbon. There's also a fully decorated Christmas tree with white lights and an assortment of silver and gold balls in the den just around the corner from this space.

I wasn't sure how to handle the ceremony design, but my brother Max helped with that since he's the one who designed the outdoor wedding pergola. For inside, we used a smaller white arched pergola with red roses and greenery for decoration. They'll marry in front of the living room fireplace. I did the runner and slipcovers for the chairs in white. Rose and green berry centerpieces sit on the buffet table and assorted end tables.

After the ceremony, the chairs will be removed to make room for a reception with champagne, appetizers, and dancing. I smile, pleased with the effect. Maybe I can add wedding decorator to my résumé after this. It's not like the home-decorating clients are lining up after my reputation was shredded. *No dwelling.* Things will get better, I assure myself.

I hear female laughter upstairs, where Paige is getting ready with her sisters, Brooke and Kayla. I don't want to interrupt sister bonding time. I head to the kitchen, help myself to a glass of water, and settle at the kitchen island. Soon the guests will arrive and the *Bride Special* crew.

Alone with my thoughts, my spirits droop as my current career woes spin round and round in my mind with no solution. My shameful secret weighs me down, and the fact that it can do that on Christmas Eve starts to make me more mad than ashamed. I know I was warm and friendly at my old workplace with everyone, but Brett, my boss's husband, took it the wrong way.

Brett often stopped by our office. One day he cornered me in the break room and told me he got my signal, that I'd been making eyes at him for years, and now was our chance.

I told him I was friendly with everyone, but he insisted

there was more between us. He boxed me in against the counter and tried to kiss me. I was so grateful when a coworker walked in on us because I was truly trapped.

I dashed toward the safety of the restroom in the hallway outside our office, shaken. And when I came out, he surprised me, coming up behind me and covering my mouth with his hand.

He whispered in my ear, "If you breathe a word of this to Tabitha, I'll say you came on to me. Your boss wouldn't like to hear that. And who would she believe? Her husband of twenty-eight years or her employee who's always so friendly with me?"

I nodded, my heart pounding.

As soon as he released me, I whirled and said firmly, "I'm not interested in you. I told you I'm friendly with everyone."

He pinched my chin. "It was different with me. Admit it."

I jerked away and rushed back to the office.

I rub my temples at the headache forming there. I was afraid to go to my boss about what happened. I wasn't sure she'd believe me, and I didn't want to set Brett off. Unfortunately, Brett couldn't seem to let go of me, and that was what finally pushed things too far with Tabitha. My gut does a slow roll, remembering. She blamed me for everything and made sure the wealthy community where I used to work turned its back on me. The social reach of those influential people has been staggering.

I blow out a breath. I need to chill before the ceremony. It starts at five, so I've got at least an hour. My little studio apartment is just down the street.

I tuck my glass into the dishwasher, go to the front hall closet for my red wool jacket, and head outside. It's a brisk late afternoon, already dark. I sing a Christmas carol to myself as I walk, trying to get back in the spirit.

A lot is wrong in my life, but there are brighter things on the horizon. I have to believe that. I'm safe back in my hometown, I've got a paycheck (for now), and I'm about to enjoy a wedding with two people I care about. There's a lot right in my life too.

And I love Christmas with all the warm cozy feelings it brings. I love the bright lights and shiny decorations, gathering with friends and family, and the message of peace and goodwill toward all of humanity. And pets! Can't forget pets. Max and Brooke's golden retriever, Scout, is a giant bundle of love for everyone he meets. My spirits lift again. When I get a place of my own, I'm definitely getting a dog.

I'm halfway home when a black pickup truck idles at the curb next to me.

I pick up speed.

The truck follows me, and the window powers down. My heart leaps into my throat.

4

Oh, it's just Gage! I've never been so happy to see him. I had Brett on my mind, but I don't think he knows I'm living in my brother's cottage, about forty minutes away from my old workplace.

Gage leans toward me. "Hey, stranger, where ya headed?" He sounds friendly.

"Hi! What're you doing here?"

"What do you think? I'm going to the wedding."

I thought it was just for immediate family and close friends. I'm only invited because of my family connection since Paige's sister Brooke married my brother Max. And the fact that I'm needed for last-minute design touches. I guess since Gage has been working for Paige and Spencer as long as I have, they included him. Come to think of it, I have heard Spencer call Gage "Williams" in that way guys have of using someone's last name to be extra friendly.

I get closer to the passenger side of his truck and take in his outfit—a black peacoat left open to reveal a sharp gray suit. I'm stunned at the transformation. The crisp white of his dress shirt makes a sharp contrast to the hint of sexy dark scruff on his jaw. My lips part, my pulse beating wildly as heat rushes through my body.

I've only ever seen him in flannel shirts and jeans. It's

hard to believe this is the same guy with inked sinewy fore-arms and a tool belt hanging low on his hips. He's like the buttoned-up version of the alpha male I know and tolerate. All that raw masculinity just waiting to be set free.

What's wrong with me? Professional boundaries. You're never putting yourself in a bad position at work ever again.

"Skylar?"

I focus on the knot of his maroon tie. "Ceremony's not for another hour."

"Yeah, I got here too early. I left extra time for traffic from Jersey, but there wasn't any."

"Well, it is Christmas Eve. I suppose most people are already where they want to be."

"Where were you walking off to?" He gestures in the opposite direction. "Wedding's that way."

"I was just going to chill at my apartment for a bit. It's that small studio behind the cottage at the end of the street."

"Mind if I join you?"

My throat goes dry. Normally I'd be welcoming, but I work with him, and that was also before he turned so panty-melting hot. Okay, I can admit it. There's something extra sexy about a powerful muscular man wrapped in a suit. It's like he's barely contained and I need to strip him bare to set him free. *Eep!* He's shifted from the *throw him in a volcano* list to the *can't stop looking at him* list. But he's bad for me like a giant greasy burger.

Let's put him on the junk-food list.

"C'mon, it's Christmas Eve," he says with a smile that steals my breath. I don't think I've ever seen him smile before. "I promise not to be difficult."

I'm not getting a creeper vibe from him. On the contrary, I'm irresistibly drawn in.

"Sure." My voice sounds breathy, and I force a cool profes-sional tone. "Though I have to warn you my fridge is empty."

"No problem. Get in."

I pull open the door, hitch up my tight green velvet dress and climb in. I'm instantly enveloped by warmth and his masculine scent, woodsy and fresh. His gaze falls to my exposed bare thighs, and I wriggle my dress down to a decent level. I'm not inviting any attention.

He clears his throat. "So all this time you've been living right down the street. How did I not know that?"

I put my seatbelt on, finding that averting my eyes from his hotness makes conversation easier. "Guess you never took the time to have an actual conversation with me. You're not much of a talker except when it comes to shooting down my ideas."

He's quiet.

I risk a look at him. One corner of his mouth lifts, and my stomach flutters. Ooh, this is not good.

"Okay, truce," he says. "We're both off duty until after the New Year."

"What do you usually do on Christmas Eve?"

"Normally I have my little sister over, and we watch *Die Hard* while stuffing ourselves with Christmas cookies. She bakes four different kinds. Then she makes me watch some godawful kiddy Christmas specials featuring talking reindeer, a snowman, and a dog. That kind of thing."

My heart squeezes. He's so sweet to his little sister. "You mean Rudolph, Frosty, and Snoopy?"

"Yeah."

He puts the truck in gear and drives down the street. Okay, he's officially moved from the *junk food* list to the *I think I like him* list. Just as a respectful coworker from a professional distance. To think before today he was on the volcano list!

"Do you open presents at midnight or the next day?" I ask.

"I let her open one gift at midnight and then a pile the next morning."

He sounds more like a dad than a big brother. What about their parents? "What's she doing tonight?"

"She wanted to go to her new boyfriend's Christmas Eve party at his parents' house. I met the guy earlier today. I put a little fear into him, but ya know, goes with the big-brother territory."

"How old is she?"

"Twenty-one."

Overprotective big brother—check. That's not necessarily a bad thing. I'm sure he does it out of love like my brothers.

"What about your parents?" I ask. "Are they still, uh, around?"

His jaw tightens. "They're not part of our lives anymore."

"But they're still alive?"

"Last I heard."

Seems like a sore subject, so I don't pry. We don't know each other well enough for that. After all, the most I knew about him before today was that he stuck rigidly to his construction schedule and budget. And was completely unreasonable. Tonight he seems different, mellower.

He parks at Max's place. Then he shocks me by getting out, jogging around the truck, and opening my door. He offers his hand to help me out.

"Thanks," I mumble, unused to a guy being so solicitous. And I certainly never expected it from Mr. Grumps here. Let's chalk it up to Christmas magic.

Because if he's suddenly panty-melting hot *and* perfect boyfriend material, I don't know how to reconcile that with all the agitation of working with a completely unreasonable, rigid, aggravating man. I suppose it's possible he was always this gorgeous, but my irritation blinded me to it. That actually makes a lot of sense. Personality flaws can definitely make a person seem less attractive and, boy, does he have a lot of them.

Sky, you are not giving him even the smallest window to bad-mouth you for any reason. This is a work colleague. Consider this the office Christmas party.

We walk down the stone pathway to the studio.

"I'm actually not off duty," I say, emphasizing my professional work mode. "I decorated for the wedding, and I have to make sure it stays looking good throughout. *Bride Special*—that's a major bridal magazine—will be there to feature the wedding in an article."

"I'd never want that."

I unlock the door, step inside, and flip on the light. "Want what? The wedding or the article?" I kick off my green pumps by the door, pleased that he's about to say something that reveals his personality flaws once more, which will scale down the hotness factor. Like he's opposed to marriage or the idea of commitment. *Go ahead, Gage. Share away!*

He doesn't share. Instead he quietly surveys the space, taking in the small galley kitchen and the large open living area. Max moved my stuff here for me—a purple chenille sofa, geometric gray and green area rug, and assorted mismatched end tables. The coffee table is a large tray on metal legs. All of my furniture is from sales at wholesale stores where I shop for clients. There's also an architect drafting table in the back of the space for Brooke's work. She uses this as her home office.

While he's busy studying my temporary place, I go to the kitchen and get him a glass of water, figuring I'll be a good host with what I have on hand. Also, I'm nervous and I don't know why. It's not like I haven't spent plenty of time with him. Even some of it just the two of us as we stepped to a quieter space to argue over design changes for the restaurant.

When I turn from the sink, he's leaning against the counter a short distance away, his jacket casually slung over one arm.

I'm suddenly hyperaware of him and of me. A rare self-consciousness takes over, and I suddenly don't know if I should stand straight or lean like he is, or maybe sit? I hand him the glass of water. "Here you go. So back to our previous conversation, what is it you don't like—the wedding at the inn or the magazine covering it?"

He takes a drink of water, his Adam's apple moving up and down in his throat. That tie needs to be loosened, the top button undone to expose more skin. My mouth goes dry at the thought.

Stop undressing him with your eyes! Now listen close, he's about to tell you why he's the worst person in the world to ever get involved with. Be smart. Be on guard.

He lowers his glass and sets it on the counter. "I'd never want to be the focus of a magazine."

He's not anti-marriage, which means he's pro commitment. Dammit. He's still in captivating territory.

"Totally agree on the magazine," I say. "For me, I'd want a huge wedding with all the works."

His eyes widen in apparent horror at the thought.

I relax. See, he's just another one of those commitment-phobes. "Not like it's happening anytime soon, but now that I've decorated for their wedding, I have all sorts of ideas for what I could do with a larger palette."

He grunts in response.

We stare at each other for a moment, and it almost feels like we've drawn closer together, though neither of us has moved. His dark brown eyes seem warmer. I worry my lower lip, and his gaze drops to my mouth. A low ache in my belly spurs me into action, getting a glass of water for myself while I tell myself to look at him objectively. He's horrified by the wedding idea, not just the magazine covering it, so that makes things easy. Now pretend you're at the office Christmas party!

I take a long drink of water. "So is this the relaxed Gage I never get to see at work?"

He cracks a smile. "You tell me."

"Definitely." I incline my head toward the living room. "Let's take a seat."

He strides over to the sofa and sits, leaving his jacket on the end of the arm. Then he takes off his gray blazer and puts that on top. I have a sudden vision of him slowly untying his tie, then the buttons on his shirt, exposing more muscular tanned chest. Does he have ink on his chest?

I grab the remote and turn the TV on to a Christmas music channel for relaxing ambiance. Then I join him on the sofa, careful to sit a distance away. There's a whole cushion between us.

"Cool that your brother lets you crash here," he says.

Look at that. He's actually trying to make conversation. Usually I get grunts and sharp denials. An occasional "Miss Perky" said in an amused voice like he doesn't take me seriously. Just like my brothers. They think I'm the definition of free spirit, light and airy, and maybe I am. But I can also be serious when something's important to me like my career. I get worked up just thinking about that hot mess.

I set my glass on the coffee table and say stiffly, "This is a temporary living situation for when I work in Summerdale."

He lifts his brows. "Did I say something wrong?"

"You shouldn't call me Miss Perky anymore. I have my serious moments."

"Then you shouldn't call me Mr. Grumps. I have my lighter moments."

"No, you don't."

He cocks his head. "Didn't you just say over in the kitchen there that I seem relaxed?"

I twist my mouth to the side. He's right. I'm just cranky over my situation. "Okay, from now on, no more Mr. Grumps."

"Thanks, Miss Perky."

I narrow my eyes.

A rusty sound emerges from his chest that might actually be a laugh. "What? I didn't say I wouldn't call you Miss Perky. You're the definition of perky except when you're mad like right now. Come on, how can you be mad when 'Jingle Bell Rock' is on?"

I slouch into the cushions, close my eyes, and take in the music. I let my senses come to the forefront—the softness of the chenille fabric under me, the cheerful sound of Christmas music, the scent of woodsy man. My eyes fly open, and I leap off the sofa.

"Where're you going?" he asks with a note of bewilderment.

"I'm getting my aromatherapy diffuser. I think nutmeg essential oil will be just the thing."

His brows lift.

I go to the small bedroom in back and gather the diffuser and pick out the nutmeg essential oil from my collection. I like to set this on a timer with lavender essential oil for bedtime. I return and set the diffuser on the coffee table and get to work setting it up.

"You really are a hippie," he says.

I flop back on the sofa. "Well, I come by it legitimately. My grandfather was one of the original hippies in the sixties who founded Summerdale. He helped build the lake house I grew up in."

"You grew up here?"

"Yeah. I moved to Connecticut for work, but the lake house was always home." I sigh. "Well, it was until my brother Max had to sell it."

He's quiet, listening intently.

This has been bothering me for so long I feel compelled to share, especially since moving back to town brings back all the memories. "After Mom died, my two older brothers and I inherited the lake house. Liam, that's my oldest brother, needed money to save his farm and because he had a pregnant live-in girlfriend. Being a dad, he wanted to do right by them, so he asked Max to sell our place, and he did."

"No one asked you?"

I swallow hard over the lump of emotion lodged in my throat. "I wasn't part of the equation, but why should I be? I was doing just fine at the time, and Liam really needed the money. I gave my blessing and said 'We just gotta trust the universe.'"

He jabs a finger at me. "Now that's where it sucks being a hippy. If that house meant a lot to me, I would've fought for it."

"Family first. It's just me and my brothers now. I'm not going to turn my back on a brother in need."

"*You* didn't get his girlfriend pregnant."

I shoot him a look. "And your point is?"

"Guy's got to take some responsibility."

"He did, but his hay farm was in trouble after he went pesticide-free and everything died, so he had to replenish the soil with animals and start again. He was trying to do a good thing. And now I'm an aunt! That's the best part. He had twins, a boy and a girl—Max and Willow."

He gives me a pointed look. "He named his kid after your brother."

I read in his implied *and not you*. "That's because Max was living in our lake house, and it was hard for him to move out because he was very attached to it. Anyway, he had to crash on someone's couch until he bought this place."

He leans back in his seat. "Sure. It's just odd to have two Maxes in the family. Uncle and nephew. Wasn't a comment on you."

"Oh." I close my eyes and breathe in the warm scent of nutmeg in the air, telling myself to relax. I don't know why Gage makes me so defensive. He's not judging me. This is just his way of making conversation.

"Can I see your lake house? I'm curious which one it is. I've seen a lot of nice houses around the lake."

My throat tightens, and I can't bring myself to say the truth. The new owner demolished the small cottage I loved, that my grandfather built, in favor of a modern, boxy two-story white house. The new house sticks out and hogs the view of the lake from the neighbors. I hate it. "We should probably get over to the wedding."

He gestures to the diffuser with puffs of steam coming out of the top. "But we were just starting to mellow with this thing." He leans toward me, his voice soothing. "If I hit a tender spot, you can just change the subject. No need to run off."

I nod, but inside I'm shocked at his perceptiveness. I just assumed with his gruff manner that he wouldn't be tuned into emotions at all.

I smile and hop up. "Good news. I made cookies."

"For real? Aw, man, I was missing Livvie's cookies this year."

I practically skip to the kitchen, pleased I can bring some Christmas cheer to our little office party. I grab the plate of cookies from the counter, where I left them last night, and carry them in.

I whip off the plastic covering and present him with the plate.

His mouth screws up. "They're orange."

"They're carrot cookies."

He takes a small bite and chews, making all sorts of strange faces. "Are those raisins in there?"

"Yeah, carrot raisin cookies." My shoulders droop. "You don't like them?"

"Who makes healthy cookies for Christmas?"

"What's wrong with healthy cookies?"

He looks toward the kitchen longingly. "Don't you have anything with sprinkles or chocolate chips?"

I take a bite of cookie. "Delicious. Try it again. You barely took a bite."

He takes another bite and chews ferociously. "Lotta carrot in there."

"Some zucchini too."

He grimaces. "I have to introduce you to Livvie. She'll set you straight on a proper Christmas cookie."

"Hey, you wanted a Christmas cookie, I gave you one. Homemade last night."

"Thank you." But it sounds like *please, no more*.

I huff. "Wasted on you." I cover the plate and put it back in the kitchen. Then I just stand there for a moment, resting my hands on top of the counter and bowing my head. Nostalgia's getting to me again. Mom used to make these cookies for every special occasion. I miss her so much. She understood me. She loved that I was creative. She probably would've been more like that too if she didn't have to work and raise us three kids. Dad left when I was little, but he was never much help anyway.

"Skylar."

He's right behind me. I blink back tears, trying not to let them roll down my cheeks. "Yes?"

"I didn't mean to insult your cookies."

I turn and wave that away. "Mom's recipe. We had them on every holiday. I know not everyone likes raisins in their cookies. Don't worry about it."

"Or vegetables." At my annoyed look, he adds, "To each his own. Maybe I'll try another one. They could grow on me."

He reaches past me to the plate on the counter, bringing our bodies so close I can feel his heat. His gaze meets mine, a dark smolder that makes every nerve ending stand on end. My breath hitches.

"Gage," I whisper on a shaky breath, half wanting to shift away and half wanting to close the distance. My heart pounds against my rib cage.

He backs away. "Yeah, who am I kidding? Not for me." He rubs the back of his neck and turns away. "We should get to the wedding. I'm sure they're wondering where you are, probably want to interview you or something."

He's at the front door before I can say another word.

Did we just have a moment?

5

Gage

At the wedding ceremony, Skylar and I sit on opposite sides of the aisle, which means I have a clear view—the curve of her cheek, the silky shine of her dark hair, the pink of her lips. I need to stop looking so much.

Skylar catches my eye. *Busted!* I jerk my chin at her and face front.

Just the short time I spent with her outside of work revealed a whole different side to her. I always knew she had hippy tendencies, but she can also be vulnerable and serious too. She's complex.

I force myself to pay attention to the ceremony in an effort to ignore Skylar. Mayor Levi Appleton is presiding, a young guy for a mayor, thirty at most, but I hear he's from one of the founding families here, so everyone knows him. The photographer from *Bride Special* keeps snapping pictures, her flash going off throughout the ceremony. Paige and Spencer are so lost in each other's eyes they don't seem to notice the camera flash. Their golden retriever, Bear, is dressed for the occasion with a black bow tie around his neck, along with his "cousin" golden retriever, Brooke's dog Scout. Both dogs are lying down at the end of the aisle with a brunette woman I don't know holding their leashes.

Skylar blinks rapidly during the vows like she's trying not to cry. My sister does that move too, and it never works. Not that I'm staring at Skylar. I just noticed while I was casually looking around. Is she that sensitive, or is she close with Paige?

"I now pronounce you husband and wife," Levi says.

Spencer cradles Paige's face in both hands and kisses her tenderly. Everyone cheers. Someone hoots in the background.

They walk down the small aisle, both of them beaming, and something in the vicinity of my heart shifts uncomfortably. I'm not against marriage per se, but it's hard not to consider the odds of success and find it daunting. Two of my best friends from home are already divorced, and they were pathetic messes during the process.

With one glaring exception, I've stayed far away from the messy emotion of love. Now I keep everything in my life in order precisely to my standards. Much simpler that way.

Skylar throws an arm around the teary brunette who was holding Bear's leash. Now he's roaming free, sniffing interesting spots on the floor and on people. "Audrey, you'll have to join me in the single-girl club. We'll have our own fun."

Audrey sighs and wipes her eyes. "Another friend bites the dust. Married love dust that is."

I look away so it's not obvious I'm eavesdropping. I'm just curious what Skylar's like in a social situation, that's all. At work she's nothing but a headache, always bugging me for changes I don't want to make.

"How's your book coming along?" Skylar asks.

Audrey presses her lips together. "It's coming, I guess. I work on it every day, early morning and late at night. I'm in the middle of the story and wondering how the hell I got there. I'm starting to worry it's all just terrible."

Paige arrives and hugs them both. Okay, I may be peeking while I eavesdrop.

I shift to an inconspicuous place by the fireplace. It's not like I know that many people here. Just Spencer, who's surrounded by people, and Paige and Brooke, who hired me to work on the inn and the restaurant. Actually, I know

Brooke's younger sister, Kayla, and her older brother, Wyatt. Brooke's husband, Max, too. And isn't that the older woman who welcomed me to town across the room? Mrs. Ellis. Guess I know more people than I realized.

"You have to finish your book," Paige tells Audrey. "I insist. This is your book baby."

"So this is what it feels like to give birth," Audrey quips. "It's rougher than I thought."

Wyatt joins them with his hugely pregnant wife, a pretty woman with long auburn hair, wearing a purple sweater dress that emphasizes her curves, especially the baby bump.

"I wish it were that easy," his wife says. "That's not the word in my childbirth class."

"You should see the video we had to watch," Wyatt says enthusiastically. "Terrifying. I mean it looks *impossible*—"

His wife shoots him a dark look.

"I don't think Sydney wants to hear that right now," Audrey says gently.

Spencer approaches me and slaps me on the back. He's around my age with short brown hair and a trimmed beard. Newly married and beaming. "Williams! How're you doing?"

"I'm great. Congratulations."

"Thanks. Couldn't be happier. And it's good for the inn, too, to have the magazine people here. Really puts us on the map. Not only that, my brilliant wife—ha! never thought I'd say wife, look at me already saying wife. Anyway, Paige arranged for an article in *Leisure Travel* magazine next summer, featuring an elopement wedding. We just need to find the perfect couple for that. Know anyone?"

I straighten to my full height. "Me? No."

"Well, we've got six months. Something will come up. And it'll be just in time to show off Spencer's." That's the restaurant I'm building from scratch in the space next to the inn.

"That's great. Really happy for you."

"Wish I had more jobs to give you. After our home renovation, we're all set. It's cool to have another alpha boss around." He winks. "That's what my wife calls me, and you seem the same way since you get the job done to high standards and never take offense to my tone." He lowers his voice. "Whatever my *tone* is."

I shrug. I never noticed a tone. He tells me what needs doing, and I make sure it gets done exactly right.

Paige appears at his side with two champagne glasses. "You know perfectly well when you're stepping into arrogant-boss territory. You get a tone."

"Takes one to know one," Spencer returns with a lovesick smile. They clink glasses and kiss, not bothering to drink.

"Time for the champagne toast," Kayla announces, gesturing to two tables with champagne waiting.

After everyone gets a glass, the best man, one of Spencer's longtime friends from home, delivers a toast. "To the happy couple, Paige and Spencer. Thank God you found him, Paige. No one else could've reformed him like you did."

"Ha-ha," Spencer says.

Paige holds up her glass. "I'll drink to that!"

"Cheers, everybody," the best man says.

Everyone takes a drink.

"Help yourself to the delicious food," Kayla announces, gesturing to the jam-packed reception table. "All Spencer's cooking, so you know it's amazing!"

The photographer dashes over first to take pictures of the food. It'll probably look great in the magazine.

I get in line with the crowd for food. I thought it was going to be just appetizers. I guess when you have a chef for a groom, things can get out of hand. On one end of the table is a full prime rib with an attendant carving it for guests. Then there's lasagna, bread baked into the shape of a star with parmesan cheese sprinkled on top, two huge bowls of salad, and, strangely, a pyramid stack of tamales. Doesn't seem like wedding food to me.

There's also meat pies covered in cheese, quiche, and mini pizzas. A table across the room holds warm cider, coffee, tea, and an assortment of tiny pastries on platters. In the center is the wedding cake, a traditional three-tiered white cake with decorative icing flowers on top and around the edges. Hold on. Is that a platter of Christmas cookies? The good kind with chocolate chips and red and green sprinkles?

My stomach growls.

"Try the tamales. Best thing here," a voice says from behind me.

I turn to see Paige's older brother, Wyatt, with a middle-aged guy with thinning blond hair bowing his head bashfully. I've met Wyatt a few times, as he likes to do surprise pop-ins to inspect the work we're doing on the restaurant. It drives Paige crazy when she catches him. I get it. He's a big brother like me who takes his job seriously, looking out for his younger sisters.

Wyatt smirks at the embarrassed-looking guy. Word is, Wyatt is a retired tech billionaire. The guy's in his thirties with thick brown hair and brown eyes. I can see the family resemblance to his sisters. "Your tamales should be the center-piece of every special occasion—holidays, birthdays, weddings. Any damn day." He turns to me. "Gage, meet Bill, postman by day, tamale chef extraordinaire by night."

"Nice to meet you. I'll definitely try one."

"Try three," Wyatt says.

The tips of Bill's ears turn red. They chat about tamales and a food truck that Wyatt wants to get for him down by Lake Summerdale.

We move up in line to get our food. After Bill gets his food and steps out of line, Wyatt says to me, "Isn't this town great?"

"That's what I keep hearing."

"You should consider a relocation," he says. "I've got lots of contacts I could refer you to."

"Thanks, but I'm fine where I'm at in Jersey."

"Hey, I'm from New Jersey too, and it has its appeals, but you can't get better than a town that has—" Wyatt ticks off on his fingers "—a landlocked lighthouse, a tamale-delivering mailman, and a grocery store owner who could be Santa's doppelganger."

I have no idea what to say to that. Not exactly what I look for in a town. And isn't Santa just a guy dressed in a suit?

"Think about it," he says.

"Are you on the welcoming committee too?"

His brown eyes widen. "There's a welcoming committee? How come I was never welcomed? I'm a recent resident."

I look around. "That woman over there. Mrs. Ellis. She welcomed me and asked a bunch of questions to get to know me. Apparently, they do something on your birthday."

He looks over at her. "Well, I guess that's who I'll need to talk to about this welcome business. Geez, and here I've been singing Summerdale's praises to anyone who'll listen and I wasn't even properly welcomed. I even got all three of my sisters to move here!"

He takes his full plate and meets up with his wife standing nearby, who flashes a cheeky smile. "I'd say I properly welcomed you, *Satan*," she says.

He flashes a smile and then gets serious, saying in a firm voice, "We're three weeks away from full term. You need to get off your feet and eat."

"I'm fine." Still, she lets him guide her to a chair in the corner.

Several guys clear the rows of chairs from the wedding to make room for people to mingle during the reception. I'm impressed with how quiet and efficient they are.

I help myself to extra tamales and head over to stand by a round table in the corner near the kitchen. It does look good in here. Skylar managed to make it look both festive for Christmas, yet still wedding-like with the touches of white and gold. She knows her stuff. I look around for her and find her chatting with Mrs. Ellis and the mayor, Levi. My shoulders tense. That guy looks awfully interested in what Skylar's saying. I don't want to watch a guy pick up Skylar.

I shift to the den, where there's a smaller crowd. I stick around there even after I hear the music start up in the next room. Dancing is not my thing.

Mrs. Ellis appears in the archway of the room, her gaze narrowing on me. I suddenly have the urge to escape. *I don't need to be welcomed anymore, thanks.*

She walks over to me, limping a little like she has a bad

hip. She's dressed nice in a dark red dress cinched with a belt, a sparkling Christmas wreath pin on her chest. Her shoes are thick-soled black flats.

"Merry Christmas, Gage," she says. "Why're you hiding in here?"

She remembered my name. "I'm not hiding."

"Seems you haven't been properly welcomed by our community." She shifts closer and looks up at me. "Dance with me, please."

It's not a question.

"Uh, I'm not much for dancing, ma'am. Thank you anyway."

"Then now's the perfect time to learn," she says with an edge to her voice that has me standing straighter. Is she going to yell at me if I don't agree? I'm getting flashbacks to my school days. Skylar did say Mrs. Ellis was her strict third-grade teacher.

I walk with her toward the living room. "I didn't know the welcoming committee would be here too."

"I'm at every important occasion."

"Just you?"

"The others had previous commitments. I'm the head of the committee. Between you and me," she says in a loud conspiratorial tone, "I'm pretty sure I was only invited to the wedding because of my famous granddaughter, Harper Ellis. She helped launch the inn just by showing up opening weekend with her famous actress friend and their royal husbands."

"Cool." Then I add just to be polite, "I'm sure you were invited for other reasons too."

We reach the dance floor, and she puts my hand on her waist and takes my other hand in hers. Her hand goes to my shoulder. "This is a box step," she says. "Pay attention."

"I know how to dance." My sister forced me to practice with her before her first formal. "I just don't enjoy it."

"Work on that attitude," she says. "It can be a real downer."

My mind flashes to Skylar, who once told me to drop the

'tude. I seem to be stuck on thoughts of Skylar today. I refocus on Mrs. Ellis and try to find something to talk about. Oh yeah, she mentioned her famous granddaughter and a royal husband. Oh wow, I actually know that name. Harper Ellis was in this awesome thriller I saw recently.

"Your granddaughter is the Harper Ellis in *Dark Blade*?"

"That's her. She was a real badass in that one." She smiles proudly. "Her husband, Garrett, is part of the royal Rourke family."

"No wonder you're the head of the welcoming committee. You're famous by association."

"That and my charm," she says with a smile that almost makes her seem nice. Otherwise, she looks (and sounds) like she'd snap your head off if you crossed her or disappointed her in any way. "How're you liking Summerdale?"

"Well, it's the first place I've heard of that delivers tamales with your mail."

"Oh, we're much more than that. This is a real community. Everyone knows everyone, and if they don't, they try to get to know them. We love to get together on the regular. There's Winterfest, Spring Carnival, the end-of-summer regatta on the lake, and the Fall Harvest Festival. Not to mention weddings, birthdays, and holidays. When you're here, you're home, and there's lots of opportunities to get to know your neighbors. Where do you live?"

"New Jersey. About an hour and a half from here."

"Own or rent?"

"Proud homeowner. Fixed it up myself." *She sure asks a lot of personal questions.*

"A good sign. My son-in-law is a great fixer too." She looks around and then barks across the room, "Skylar, ask Levi to dance."

Skylar freezes where she's standing with Audrey and Levi. Levi makes the move and asks her, offering his hand.

Next thing I know, they're slow dancing right next to us.

I'm suddenly tense. Levi's hands are on Skylar's waist, spanning widely like he's trying to feel more of her curves. *Give her some space, man.*

"Are you okay, Gage?" Mrs. Ellis asks. "You seem distracted."

I focus on her, but I can still see Skylar and Levi in my peripheral vision, dancing too close. "Fine."

"You don't seem fine."

"I'm just not into dancing all that much. In fact—"

"I'm starting to feel it in my hip." She turns to Levi. "Help me back to my seat. Skylar, take my place with Gage."

Skylar's hand goes to her throat, her blue eyes wide. "Oh, he doesn't...that's not." She coughs. "I'll help you to your seat, Mrs. Ellis."

Levi offers Mrs. Ellis his arm in a gallant gesture and escorts Mrs. Ellis to a cushioned chair, the only one in the space, so I'm guessing it was put there for her.

Skylar bites her lower lip and speaks to my chest. "We don't have to—"

"That woman seems determined to set you up with someone. First Levi, then me."

She steps closer, lowering her voice and meeting my eyes. A jolt goes through me the moment our eyes meet up close. "I know, right? I'm starting to think it's Mrs. Ellis who needs a companion. Male, female, different species, I'm not sure, but she's lived alone far too long."

I burst out laughing. "Another species?"

She smiles, her blue eyes sparkling. "I've never seen you laugh like that before."

"You've never seen me do lots of things before."

Pink rushes to her cheeks. "I guess that's true." She smooths her hair, brushing it back over her shoulder.

"I thought Mrs. Ellis was married."

"Widowed. Anyway, I didn't mean like an alien species, I meant a pet."

"Pets are a lot of responsibility."

"I've heard of this stuffed companion cat you can buy that's soft and furry like the real thing. And it even purrs."

I stare at her. She's unlike anyone I've ever met, from the way she dresses to the thoughts in her head, but she's kind. I appreciate that rare quality in a person. "You want to set her up with a stuffed animal?"

"More like a robot pet."

"Sounds high tech for someone her age."

We both look over to Mrs. Ellis, who's working her cell phone like a pro, tapping and swiping. Maybe she's more with it than I thought.

Skylar and I look at each other, both of us fighting a laugh.

"She's probably on Tinder right now," I whisper.

She grabs my arm and cracks up.

I grin. I like to see her happy. It makes me feel happy, and that's not a feeling I often have.

My heart pounds as I consider this next step. I know better than to mix business with pleasure, but it's a wedding, and we're both off duty.

I lift a palm. "Should we dance? I mean, we are here."

"And there is music," Skylar says, stepping closer.

I breathe in her warm spice scent, a rush of raw lust taking me by surprise. Was this always here? Is that why I avoided dealing with her as much as possible at work?

I take her hand in mine, the fit perfect. Before we can start dancing, the music cuts out, and Kayla speaks through a microphone, announcing it's time for the cutting of the cake.

Skylar pulls her hand from mine. "Another time."

I'm disappointed, even though I didn't want to dance in the first place. Mrs. Ellis dragged me out here. "Later."

I walk back toward the quiet of the den.

A firm hand grabs my arm from behind before I can make it through the archway. I turn to find Skylar looking peeved at me. "What?"

"*Later?* You couldn't stand next to me and talk like a normal person at a wedding?"

I'm not normal?

I look toward the ceiling in an effort to keep calm. *Is that mistletoe?*

She tosses her long wavy hair over one shoulder and parks a hand on her hip. "Nothing to say? I mean, I'm as tolerant as the next person, but your attitude is sorely lacking any kind of social finesse. You literally just asked me to dance, and just because the music ended—"

"We're under the mistletoe." I lean down toward her ear, amused by her righteousness and choice of words. *Who says social finesse?* At the same time, I'm turned on. "Kiss me."

I hear her sharp intake of air just before she asks softly, "For real?"

I tuck a lock of her hair behind her ear, my spontaneous idea morphing into an urgent need. "It's bad luck not to. You must be into that kind of superstitious stuff." Skylar is the definition of bohemian hippie. Also, the definition of chaos, but that doesn't concern me right now.

Her brows scrunch together. "I don't understand you. First, let's dance, then the brush-off, and then *kiss me*?" Her voice hits a high note. "You're one clueless alpha, I'll say that much."

"Thank you." I gesture to the mistletoe. "If we're not within a short window of time, I'm not sure it'll count."

She sighs dramatically. "Fine." She kisses my cheek.

"We're still under the mistletoe."

She blinks a few times, and before she has a chance to fire another insult my way, I lean close, a breath away. "This is what normal people do. Like me."

"Oh," she says on a shaky breath.

I cup her jaw, the skin so soft there I have to stroke it with my thumb. This feels right, and I can't believe it took me so long to get here. Every cell in my body vibrates in anticipation, my gut tightening, my pulse rushing. There's nothing but this intense pull to get closer, the world fading away.

I jump back in shock as a golden retriever muzzle pokes between my legs. It's Scout, Brooke's dog.

I shove him away with a grumble of warning.

Skylar lets out a shaky laugh and gives me a little wave before hightailing it back to the action by the wedding cake.

I walk into the den and flop down in the recliner. It's for the best. What was I thinking? I know better than to get involved with someone I work with. And Skylar seems like the type of woman who'd not only want a relationship, she'd want to *talk* about the relationship. Not my strong suit. I'd only end up hurting her.

I'm sure once Skylar starts making her usual unreasonable demands at work, all of this…chemistry will die down. It was just the heat of the moment. An intimate Christmas Eve wedding could make even the most jaded bachelor consider getting some of that love feeling for himself.

No, that can't be it. I don't want love. It must've been lust.

Though I've never felt lust so powerful come on so suddenly. Like the floodgates opened after a long buildup.

I scrub a hand over my face. I need to get out more.

6

Skylar

You know when you have a romantic misstep like, say, you almost kiss the man who makes your work life aggravating just because it's Christmas Eve and you're at a wedding and there's mistletoe?

Well, that wasn't *my* idea. I mean, yes, they say opposites attract, so maybe for a brief teensy-tiny moment I was attracted to Gage and vice versa. But nothing happened. Thank God. Last thing I need is to cross the line in the workplace and get burned again. My professional reputation can't take any more damage.

The problem is, ever since I got back to work after the holidays, Gage acts like I don't exist. If I thought he was stone cold before, now he's ice. He never looks directly at me, and when forced to talk to me, he asks me to text him about the issue to get away from me as fast as possible. Sure he's busy, but this is the job. As the contractor, he's required to talk to everyone working on the project.

He doesn't even call me Miss Perky anymore. He doesn't call me anything at all.

So today I'm going to break the ice. I have a handy excuse. Last night at the Winterfest meeting, Mrs. Ellis asked me to pass on a birthday cupcake to Gage on behalf of the welcoming committee. That committee is new. The strange thing was, when I asked to join, she said they weren't taking new members. She wouldn't even tell me who was on the committee. Not very welcoming for a welcoming committee. Anyway, she had a doctor's appointment, so she couldn't bring Gage the cupcake herself.

I wait until he takes a lunch break with his crew, everyone sitting on metal folding chairs at a makeshift table of a piece of plywood over two sawhorses. I join them sometimes. More often, I walk to my place down the street and get back to marketing in an attempt to drum up business. Leap and the net will appear, right? Only it hasn't. Something will turn up. I'm not admitting to my big brother Max that I failed. Not just because he'll think I was impulsive again, breezing through all my savings. He'll want to get involved, and it'll only make things so much worse.

I carefully take the cupcake from its plastic container, tuck it behind my back, and head over to Gage.

He sits at the head of the table, quietly eating a roast beef sandwich while the four guys on crew talk and laugh amongst themselves.

"Hey, Gage, I heard it's your birthday," I say.

The guys stop talking to listen.

Gage looks directly in my eyes for the first time in forever, and a flutter low in my belly ensues. *Cause, effect.* I really need to stop replaying that almost kiss in my head. Somehow my body's anticipating it again. It's so hard to deny my natural instincts, but this is my life now—cool professional all the way. "Who told you that?"

My cheeks flush. "The welcoming committee." I turn to the eavesdropping guys just for a break from the intensity of Gage's dark eyes. "Big day," I tell them. I pull the cupcake from behind my back with a flourish, thankful for the witnesses who will keep me from doing something impulsive like finish that almost kiss. Just so I can stop thinking about it.

Gage stares at the cupcake. It's chocolate fudge icing on a

vanilla cupcake. There's even rainbow sprinkles. If anything could bring a smile to someone's face, it's this cupcake.

I smile. "Happy birthday! Should we sing to him?" I gesture to the guys, who launch into a cheerful rendition of the "Happy Birthday" song. I join in.

Gage gestures for them to stop. Doesn't work.

Once the song ends, I try to hand him the cupcake, but he won't take it. Is it because he thinks it's from me? My gut does a slow roll. Maybe he's been avoiding me, not because of a romantic misstep, but because he doesn't like me. Which is unfair. Just because I didn't like him from day one is no reason for him not to like me. I've been nothing but professional. With the occasional outburst of temper. He really could test a saint. And here I was thinking he qualified for the *I think I like him* list. I never should've moved him from the *toss in a volcano* list. Somehow the idea doesn't make me feel better.

I try again. "It's from Summerdale Sweets. I hear everything they make is amazing." My voice sounds so forlorn I get mad at myself. He could at least be gracious enough to accept a damn birthday cupcake.

"I don't eat sugar," he says.

My temper flares. "You were raving about your sister's Christmas cookies. You said my carrot raisin cookies were too healthy."

He holds up a finger. "Amendment. I only eat sugar on Christmas. It's not Christmas, Skylar."

I'm so tempted to squash this cupcake in his face. Instead I peel off the wrapper and take a big bite. "Mmm, delicious," I say around the cupcake. I can feel my blood sugar spiking already, the chocolate fudge icing chock-full of sugar I'm not used to.

I turn on my heel to walk off with my dignity intact, but the corner of my flowing lavender dress catches on the sharp edge of the plywood and pulls it up, halting me and giving Gage a view of my blue with white stars Wonder Woman panties. My cheeks flame. One of the guys hoots. Guess Gage wasn't the only one with a view.

I back up, yank my dress off the wood, and rush away. So much for looking professional. I'm so mortified.

"Skylar, wait," Gage calls.

No way in hell. It's bad enough I offered a cupcake he rejected—who rejects a birthday cupcake?—but to flash him and the guys is too much. So what if I'm a fan of the kickass heroine who cares deeply about people and rights wrongs everywhere she goes?

My eyes get hot. I leave the remains of the cupcake on top of the newly installed bar top and dash out the front door into the cold of a January day. There's several inches of snow on the ground and an icy wind. I don't care. I'm not going back in for my coat. I'm going to my studio apartment to work on my lunch hour like I should've done in the first place.

I move briskly down the cleared path, crossing my arms and hugging myself. At least I'm wearing my winter boots. I can handle the cold. What I can't handle is facing a bunch of hooting guys who know what my panties look like. I take off at a run.

I'm nearly at my apartment when Gage appears at my side, slightly out of breath. "Skylar."

"Go away."

"I gave the guys hell for being disrespectful. Sorry that happened."

My throat tightens. "Okay."

"I'd like the cupcake. Thank you for bringing it."

I open my unlocked front door and turn. "It's on the bar top. Happy birthday." I shut the door in his face.

I go for my laptop on the side table, determined to have some productive marketing time. I'm a solo entrepreneur now, and that means I have to hustle.

Knock, knock.

You have got to be kidding me.

"Not buying anything!" I yell. "Try the next house."

Knock, knock.

"I gave at the office!"

Crap. That sounds like I gave by offering a view of my Wonder Woman panties.

Knock, knock.

Damn, this guy's as persistent as I am. I blow out a breath and go to answer the door. "What?"

"I like superheroes too," Gage says.

I stare at him. "Okay."

"I'm wearing Superman briefs."

I glance down at his crotch, realize what I'm doing, and jerk my gaze back to his face. Heat rises off me in waves. "You're just saying that to make me feel better."

"Okay, they're more like the regular Clark Kent kind, but you know any moment I could morph into my superhero form."

I bite back a smile. "You're finally talking to me again."

He rubs the back of his neck. "I talk to you."

"No, you text me to avoid talking to me. It's the strangest work relationship I've ever had."

He meets my eyes intently. "I put in the fireplace you wanted."

I suppress a sigh. That wasn't a gesture of peace on his part. "Spencer wanted it, and Paige leaned on Spencer to set you straight." *After I went to Paige to straighten the whole thing out.*

"I'll incorporate the antique mirror over the bar."

I cross my arms. "Why're you being so nice to me all of a sudden?" *Was it my panties?* Maybe they have a secret superpower that brings alpha males to their knees. Or at least makes them more cooperative.

"Can I come in?"

I back up and gesture him inside.

He quietly shuts the door behind him and exhales sharply. "The truth is, Skylar, I can't stop thinking about that mistletoe."

My breath stutters out, my heart racing double time. For once I'm utterly speechless.

∼

Gage

I stay by the door, not trusting myself to get too close.

"What about it?" she asks after a long moment, pink flaring in her cheeks.

"You've thought about it too."

"Nope, not for one second. There was only a mistletoe tradition I chose not to partake in."

"Only because we were interrupted by a dog."

She laughs. "Sounds like every romantic moment in my life. Never quite happening."

I take a step closer. "Romantic?"

She waves airily, not quite meeting my eyes. "Everything's romantic at a Christmas Eve wedding. That's partly due to my interior design work. Great ambiance doesn't mean anything. Really. Don't give it another thought. I haven't."

Lie. I don't call her on it, though, because it's best if we both forget that moment ever happened. I wish I could.

She continues, her gaze not quite meeting mine. "I've learned my lesson. It's not worth trying to make romance happen. It either happens organically, or it doesn't. And let's face it, most guys are completely clueless when it comes to romance anyway, so why hope?"

She sounds like she still secretly hopes, and she really shouldn't. It'll only lead to disappointment. Guys don't think that way.

"Not that I mean you," she adds, slowly backing away like I'm suddenly a threat. "I just mean in general, and that mistletoe thing was like two other people in another time. Another dimension! So let's just go back to being coworkers and forget the whole thing. I already forgot it, and now you should too."

I decide to set her straight for her own good. "Romance is something women made up. Guys don't know the rules of that game, so you can't expect us to play it right."

She cocks her head. "Excuse me, but men came up with chivalry, writing poems to women's beauty and serenading them. Haven't you heard of a knight in shining armor?"

"I thought that was a fairy tale from the olden days."

Her eyes flash. "It was real. You need to brush up on your history."

"You're mad at me."

She throws her hands in the air. "You avoid me for weeks, and then you show up here expecting what exactly?"

My jaw works for a moment. "I had no expectations."

"Look, I've had enough awkward moments for today. Can you just let me get back to my marketing work? I'm trying to get my business off the ground."

"You're new at this?"

She exhales sharply. "I used to work for a major design firm, and then I decided to go out on my own, which is why I need to put in some time now getting new clients lined up. Excuse me while I get back to work."

She doesn't make any move to go to work. Instead she just stands there, looking at me expectantly. Like maybe she wants more of a response from me after I sort of avoided her for weeks for…reasons. Damn, words are not my strong suit.

I shove my hands in my pockets, deciding the truth is the best way to save our professional relationship. "I was putting some distance between us because the thoughts I've been having aren't appropriate for the workplace."

Her blue eyes widen, and she licks her lips. My gut tightens, the now familiar desire flaring to life.

I reach for the doorknob behind me. "I just want to keep things professional."

She nods vigorously. "Me too. Absolutely." She holds out her hand to shake, walking toward me, her eyes locked on mine.

Raw lust rushes through me. My mind flashes to her panties, the smooth curve of her ass, her long bare legs. The white stars on blue with a red waistband. Is there a matching bra?

She grabs my hand and shakes it. "Agreed. Goodbye, Gage. Like I said, I've got work to do."

And then she opens the door for me. I turn toward her, needing more despite everything I just said.

She holds up a palm and backs away.

She's right.

I walk out the door and tell myself to forget the almost kiss, the shock of her sexy view, and every lusty impulse that's on the verge of breaking free. We've got no future and way too much time together on the job.

7

Skylar

I'm at the Winterfest committee meeting when I get another text from my brother Max. *Just checking in to see if you have work lined up for spring. I can ask Brooke to check with her architecture clients. She has four lined up for spring and upcoming meetings with others. She's happy to assist.*

Brooke is his wife. I stifle a sigh. My big brother's check-ins are becoming a regular thing, ever since New Year's two and a half weeks ago. I know it's because he cares, but also because he thinks I'm so flighty and impulsive I always need an assist. It's Max's slow season in his landscaping business, so he has more time to worry over me right in his backyard. He also sends me links to business plans, marketing guides, and interior design articles, as if I don't already know this stuff. I've declined all help, nice as it is, because it's important I make it on my own to prove to him (and myself) that I can.

I put my phone away and read the agenda I just received for the meeting, glad for the distraction. Bad enough I can't stop thinking about Gage; now I've got Max breathing down my neck about my career. More pressure and tension is the last thing I need.

"Skylar, what exactly are you looking for in a man?"

General Joan asks, startling me from my thoughts. Yes, Mrs. Ellis has earned that nickname.

Audrey titters, and I shoot her a dark look. *Watch it, Miss Librarian, or you'll be next in Cupid's path!*

I know the answer to General Joan's question, but I don't want to admit it in front of all these people. *Romantic. Knight-in-shining-armor material.*

"I'm not looking for a man, Mrs. Ellis. How about you?" I smile sweetly. Maybe the matchmaker secretly wants her own match.

"Don't get fresh," she snaps.

I'm immediately contrite and also brought right back to third grade. I almost want to write "I will act respectful to my teacher" in my notebook one hundred times to make up for it. It wouldn't be the first time. She used to say not paying attention in class was also disrespectful.

General Joan's eyes bore into mine. "I saw you with Gage at the wedding, and I understand why he's such a problem for you. He couldn't even follow through on a simple dance. Levi, here, on the other hand." She gestures to our mayor as he's busy pulling a notepad and pen from his satchel. "A man of the first order. Now that's the kind of man you should spend more time with."

Levi's smile looks frozen in place. "Thank you, Mrs. Ellis, but—"

General Joan cuts him off. "Now, Levi, it's time you settled down. Your homework is to ask out one new woman a week until you've met your match."

Levi clears his throat and looks around the table. "Like I mentioned in my email, the budget looks good for Winterfest this year thanks to a generous anonymous donation." A small smile curves his lips. Everyone in town knows the anonymous donations always come from retired tech billionaire Wyatt Winters. It's kind of an inside joke to let Wyatt think he's still anonymous. His sisters told me all about him. "Let's get started on deco-rations."

General Joan whispers loudly to me, "If the beard is a

problem, I can talk to Levi about shaving it off. And he has no tattoos like some riffraff I know you put up with."

I stiffen and whisper back, "I wouldn't exactly call Gage riffraff."

"He looks like a hoodlum."

Audrey giggles, and Levi pretends not to have heard any of this.

"Not true," I say. "But you're right about Levi. He deserves someone special. Did you know Audrey here is single?" I gesture to where she's sitting conveniently next to Levi. "Aren't you two around the same age? Timing might be just right for something serious."

Audrey blushes, and Levi gives her a second look. *There. Problem solved.*

Drew clears his throat from his spot at the end of the table, his voice commanding as the soldier he used to be. "That's enough with the setups. Audrey has important things to do." He looks right at her. "You have that book to finish."

Glad for the change in topic, I pounce on that. "Ooh, what's it about?"

Everyone's curious, and it seems that the Levi potential date is forgotten.

Audrey smiles. "This is off-topic. We should get to the decorations. Winterfest is this weekend."

"Yes, and we need to figure out who's going to put up what," Levi says.

"I think we'd all like to hear what Audrey's book is about," Nicholas says kindly. *Dear Santa, you should ask out General Joan.* No, I can't do that to him. He's too darn sweet.

Audrey lifts a finger. "Okay, the short answer—it's a multigenerational family saga about a soldier with PTSD and her family's history as military officers."

Drew's chest puffs out. "I made some recommendations for her research."

"Which I appreciated," Audrey says, "though I am a librarian and know how to do research."

"Yes, but I gave you my *personal* recommendations," Drew says.

There's a tension in the air suddenly.

"So you did," she says quietly.

A volley of looks are exchanged around the table, each of us wondering what's going on with this dynamic. At least I am.

The rest of the meeting passes by uneventfully. Finally, we all file out of the library meeting room to the large open area of the first floor.

Levi approaches Audrey and asks, "Would you like to have dinner with me?"

Audrey's eyes go wide, and her jaw gapes.

Levi laughs. "Is it so strange to consider? Maybe Mrs. Ellis is onto something." He winks. "I'm not that hideous."

She puts her hand on his arm. "You know you're a catch."

Drew appears suddenly, standing next to Audrey and staring Levi down. "She's taken."

Audrey's head whips toward Drew's, her blue eyes lighting up. "I am?"

"Yes," Drew practically growls.

Levi lifts his palms and backs away, but I don't miss the wink he sends to General Joan on his way out the door. Hmm, Levi wasn't hurt at all. He was in on it. The general was just trying to get Drew to step up for Audrey. So tricky this lady!

I stand with Jenna, Audrey's close friend, a respectful distance away from Audrey and Drew, but still close enough to eavesdrop. Jenna is a tall, thin blonde who bakes amazing desserts at her shop, Summerdale Sweets.

Jenna whispers to me, "She's been in love with him forever. He's clueless."

"Except for when she was madly in love with my brother."

"Too bad that didn't work out," Jenna says. "Now he's happily married. Anyway, she went right back to her Drew crush, though at this point it's bordering on ridiculous. Give it up already. He can't see what's right in front of him."

There should be a guidebook for all these clueless men running around. I'd call it *The Nitwit's Guide to Women*. Hee-hee. Gage could use a copy too.

Audrey looks at Drew expectantly. He glowers down at her. They're an interesting study in contrasts—him tall and broad shouldered, her curvy and petite. His skin is several shades darker than hers, and the energy coming off him is restrained lethal compared to her restrained sweet. Well, they're both restrained at least. What would it take for each of them to let loose?

"If I'm taken, that's news to me," Audrey says pertly.

"Stay away from Levi," Drew grumbles.

Audrey's chin lifts. "Why? I've known him all my life. He's an upstanding citizen, mayor of our town, and not that I care all that much about appearances, but he's hot. Ask anyone."

"Hot," Drew echoes.

"Yes. Women like the beard and muscles look."

Drew rubs his jaw. "I could grow a beard."

"Mmm-hmm, so-o-o…"

"So what?" the clueless man asks.

Jenna shoots me an incredulous look.

"Anything you want to ask me?" Audrey asks.

"No," he says, completely blowing it.

Jenna elbows me. I shake my head.

Audrey looks so annoyed I can almost see her tapping her foot impatiently. "So you scared away a perfectly good guy, announce I'm taken when I'm most certainly not, and then you have no plans to ask me out yourself."

"We're friends, Aud."

She bares her teeth in a smile. "I'm going to take Levi up on dinner."

Drew shoves a hand in his hair and glances over at Levi, who's deep in conversation with General Joan. What are those two planning? I bet General Joan is setting up another ploy with Levi as bait. Glad I'm not part of her crafty plans.

Audrey turns to go.

"Wait!" Drew says.

She slowly turns back, a smile playing over her lips. "Yes?"

"Stop by the dojo for a free karate lesson on Wednesday."

He suddenly notices me and Jenna watching them. "You're all invited. Beginner adult class. Never hurts to learn self-defense."

"We'd love to," I say.

"Sure," Jenna says.

"I'll be there too," Audrey says through her teeth. I'm not sure if she's mad we're joining her or that Drew asked her out to a free karate lesson.

General Joan claps. "Excellent. Seems everyone got something out of tonight. I'll see you all on Saturday bright and early for setup at the lake. And, Skylar, don't give Gage a second thought. He's a dud."

"I wouldn't say a dud," I mumble. I mean, he's a bit rigid, but there's something admirable about a hardworking man with integrity. Right? He did stop by my place to make me feel better about my Wonder Woman panties peep show. And he took the time to explain he wanted to keep things professional, even though he has feelings for me he doesn't want to act on. Kinda like me.

Uh-oh. That seems like a slippery slope.

Just because he's not a dud doesn't mean we belong together. Let's not get crazy here. We're still complete opposites who clash regularly at work. I'm not risking any workplace issues. No guy is worth that.

General Joan limps out the door because of her bad hip. Nicholas offers his arm, which she ignores, but he stays by her side just in case.

Truth is, I wouldn't mind a relationship with the *right* man. I was in love once back in college. We met at Spring Carnival our senior year and fell hard. We were inseparable until graduation. I had plans to spend the summer in Kenya, building a school, and he planned to go to grad school in Michigan in the fall. He decided it was best to say goodbye rather than string things out long distance. I wished him well, even though it hurt. I had hoped we were serious enough to make it work.

Anyway, before the hurt, being in love was a warm bubbly

feeling that made me float through my days in a dreamy happy state.

Not annoyance. Or obsessively reliving near-miss romantic moments. General Joan is right. I'm not going to give Gage another thought.

≈

Gage

I'm not sure why I'm still hanging around Summerdale on my day off. I showed up early this morning at Spencer's request to build a booth for his restaurant by the lake. He wanted to offer people a sample of what was to come when Spencer's finally opens in the spring. Then I got roped into setting up tents and tables for the chocolate festival area and the tamale kiosk.

My eye catches on Skylar's dark hair bouncing in a high ponytail as she rushes around, distributing plates, cups, and plastic cutlery to each food vendor. I can't help but notice her. She stands out with her dark hair and red knitted headband and matching wool jacket.

I should go. I did my part, and I'm not even part of this quirky community. Honestly, now that I've met so many unique personalities—the tamale-delivering mailman, Santa (the man really does look like Santa), and the odd Mrs. Ellis with all her personal questions from the welcoming committee —I can see how a free spirit like Skylar fits in perfectly. She hasn't even noticed me she's so busy. Right. Time to go.

I turn and stride over to my truck. Just before I get the door open, something hits me in the back. I whirl just as another snowball comes flying toward me, hitting my shoulder.

Skylar grins. "Ha! Caught you slinking off before all the fun begins."

I scoop some snow off the ground and start shaping it in my hands as I stalk toward her.

She slowly backs up and then squeaks and runs.

I lob it at her, hitting her in the shoulder. I've got a sister, so I know not to play too rough.

"Ooh! This is war!" She dashes behind a tree and starts gathering ammunition.

I scoop a huge snowball together and hide it behind my back. "Okay, truce."

She pokes her head out. "You've got an evil look in your eyes. I don't trust that for a minute." Then she fires two snowballs at the same time with surprisingly good aim. I lunge to the side, but one still hits me in the arm.

"I'm coming for you," I growl. "No escape."

She lets out a high-pitched giggle. "You're going to wish *you* had an escape!"

I fire one to her right, and she pops out on that side to pelt me with snow. I rush right through it and raise my big snowball over her head.

"Gage! Don't you dare! My hair will be soaked, and I have to get through an entire day out here."

I back her up against the tree. "Oh, yeah? What will you give me?"

Her breath comes faster, her blue eyes bright. "Free hot chocolate."

"And?"

"I'll dance with you at the royal Winterfest ball tonight."

I make a face. "I'm not going to any ball. Don't you know me at all?"

She grabs my arm still raised over her head, and snow sprinkles down on her. She shakes her head, trying to get the snow out of it. "Cookies?"

"Keep talking."

"And, uh, a favor to be collected later."

"Can't think of anything?"

She takes off her glove and strokes my jaw. I go stock-still at the surprisingly tender touch. "I don't know you well enough to guess." And then she darts to the side and knocks the snow from my hands, laughing like an evil genius.

I find myself smiling. "What're you doing here all day for Winterfest?"

"I need to decorate the big red barn for the Dog's Got Talent contest. They need chairs set up, a judge's table, and someone to put up some paw print decorations. After that I'm free until they need setup for the coronation of King Frost and Queen Snowflake."

I don't even pause at the ridiculous king and queen names because I just want to be with her a little longer. "I could help."

"Yeah?"

"Sure."

She gestures for me to follow. "Always nice to have an extra set of hands. You can carry all the metal folding chairs in while I put up the paw prints."

"If I'd known you had a Dog's Got Talent contest here, I would've brought my dog, Ace."

"You have a dog?" she asks incredulously.

"Yes, why is that so hard to believe?"

"No reason. What kind? Is it a big, fanged hellhound?"

"What am I, the devil?"

She grins cheekily, and my chest warms. "To me you are."

"He's a French bulldog. Best dog in the world."

"What kind of tricks does he do?"

"He smiles."

She shakes her head. "I guess for you that's a rare thing."

"He's a dog. How many dogs do you know that smile? I mean really smile not just panting."

She pats my shoulder, and it warms at the spot. "Okay, you must be right. You have the only smiling dog in the world. Too bad he's not here to win first prize. Next year, huh?"

I don't reply because part of me actually wants to be here next year. With her.

～

Skylar

Gage was surprisingly helpful with setup. I suppose it's because he's used to hard physical labor. He brought in huge numbers of metal folding chairs on each trip from the storage area, balanced in both arms. That would've taken me, like, eight trips. He also set up the judges' table with Max's help.

I climb down from the short ladder and turn to them. "Thanks for the help. I certainly couldn't have done it as quickly as you two."

Gage inclines his head and shoves his hands in his pockets. He doesn't approach, and I worry that he's about to leave, but he just stands there staring at me from a distance. Maybe he wants to spend more time with me?

Max closes the distance and puts his hand on top of my head in his big-brother affectionate way. His brown hair is tousled as usual, and he's sporting a full beard, which looks good on him.

I knock his hand from my head. "Where's Brooke?" That's his other half.

"Home. She wanted extra time to work on Scout's tricks with him before the show."

"Cool."

"Yeah." He gets a serious look on his face, which makes me tense because I just know he's going to bug me about my job prospects *again*. "So when you get some time, Brooke would like to go over making a business plan with you. She recently did it for herself, so it's fresh in her mind."

I set my teeth. "Not necessary. I've got a plan."

"She's very organized and thorough. I think it could help. Just listen to her, okay?"

I don't want to be rude about his helpful wife, but the fact is Max is pushing this on me because he doesn't think I'm capable of running my own business. I'll get there.

I look into his concerned blue eyes, so like my own, and cave. He's family, and he just wants what's best for me. "Okay, I'll check in with her. Though I'm doing just fine."

"Yeah? So you found some clients?"

I glance at Gage, noticing he's listening closely, and lower my voice. "Not yet, but I know what to do, and I'm working on it."

Max studies me for a moment. "Any chance you can get your old job back?"

My temper flares. "No." Max's lack of confidence in my abilities irks me even more because there's no way in hell I'd ever go back to my old firm. My ex-boss is the one who ruined my reputation. I'll never go crawling back to her.

"Hey, Max," Gage says, surprising me. I didn't notice him approach. He turns to me. "What's up?"

"Nothing," I say.

"Just checking in to see how she's doing," Max says. "I'll catch up with you later, Sky." He grabs my head and kisses the top of it.

I sigh. Big-brother love. I adore him, but I wish he could see I'm not always flighty and impulsive. Anyone would have difficulty digging themselves out of the hole I found myself in.

Gage watches me closely. "You need a job?"

"That's what I'm working on, and I don't need Max to do it for me."

"Uh-huh. How long until the money runs out?"

I keep my mouth shut. The money is long gone.

"You did have startup money for your new business, right?"

My cheeks flush with shame. Before I knew what my ex-boss Tabitha was saying about me behind my back, I attempted to launch my new solo business with a splash and spent all the money from my share of our beloved lake house on marketing materials and one very expensive New York metro area commercial. All ruined by my former boss.

I know it's not my fault, but I still feel like a failure. Bad karma? In the past, I always gave generously to those in need. I should've taken the lake house money and given it to charity. The damage has been done, and there's nothing to do now but push forward.

Gage's brows furrow in concern. "The money's gone, isn't it? What's your plan after you finish at Spencer's?"

I look off toward the frozen lake, seriously considering

taking a page from Gage's book and grunting before walking away.

"Skylar?"

"I don't want to talk about work right now. It's Winterfest. I want to have fun."

He searches my expression. "Are you going to be okay?"

I look toward the lake. "Know how to ice skate?"

He glances that way. "Been a while, but it's probably like riding a bike."

I grab his arm. "Come on, the lake hasn't been frozen enough for skating in years."

"Let me put the ladder away first."

I stop and watch as he takes the ladder I just used and returns it to the storage area. I was so distracted by Max and thoughts of my flailing career that I completely forgot about the ladder.

Gage returns a moment later, and we head out the open barn doors.

"I'm not irresponsible," I inform him.

"Never said you were."

"I just forgot about the ladder because of Max."

"Big brothers can be a pain in the ass, huh?"

I laugh. "Do you have a big brother too?"

"Nope. I'm the pain in the ass."

I grin. "I could see that about you."

We arrive at the skate-rental area, get our skates, and then join a few families with small kids on the ice. They're barely moving with their beginner kids.

Gage skates ahead of me and then smoothly turns, skating backwards as he faces me. "It came back to me."

I make my way over to him. "I've been skating my whole life on the lake. How're you so good at it?"

"I briefly played ice hockey as a kid."

"Why'd you stop?"

He turns forward, and we skate together, farther away from the others. "Didn't have the money or a ride to the rink."

I want to ask why, but I suspect it was probably the reason

his parents aren't in his life anymore. A touchy subject. Today is just for fun. "I once dreamed of being a figure skater and going to the Olympics."

"Yeah, what stopped you?"

"Besides no money for lessons, I'd say lack of follow-through. I just like to follow my muse wherever she leads me."

"I don't have a muse."

"Circle back," I say, turning one way just as he turns the other. We make a wide circle and meet up close in the middle. My breath hitches, leaving a puff of cold in the air between us. "Are we ice dancing? Do you know how to do one of those cool swooping lifts?"

His eyes are warm on mine. "You're something."

My lips part, my heart thudding in my ears.

He takes his glove off and cups my cheek, stroking the sensitive spot under my ear with his thumb. Hot shivers race through me. He's about to kiss me right here on the ice.

"Williams!" a masculine voice barks.

"Shh, you're interrupting!" a feminine voice says.

Gage drops his hand. I turn to see Paige and Spencer.

They skate over and stop in front of us. "Was I interrupting?" Spencer asks.

Gage's expression is unreadable. "No, man. We were just—"

"Considering a complicated figure-skating move," I finish for him.

He stares at me.

"You know, the swooping lift?"

His lips curve up, his eyes dancing with amusement.

"Cool," Spencer says. "We're just sharing our good news with everyone. Paige is pregnant."

Paige beams. "Honeymoon jackpot."

Spencer's chest puffs out. "My strong swimmers."

Paige continues. "We did try a lot, and I'm sure it helped the way I tracked exactly when would be optimal."

He kisses her. "You're brilliant."

She cups his face with both hands. "You're amazing."

"I love you."

"I love you more."

"You're everything."

"You're everything plus more."

Gage and I exchange a look and try not to laugh. It's kind of weird that we're included in their oversharing baby lovefest.

"Congratulations!" I say, interrupting their whispered compliments to each other.

They both smile widely. I hug Paige and then Spencer. Gage shakes Spencer's hand and gives Paige a kiss on her cheek with a grumbled, "Congrats."

"Oh, there's Audrey!" Paige says, waving to her. "Let's tell her next." She turns to us. "Have fun, you two. Glad to see you're finally getting along."

They skate away.

Suddenly it feels awkward to be out here on the ice with Gage. The almost-kiss moment replaced by the reminder that we normally don't get along.

"Race you," I say and take off to the far shore of the lake. I learned a thing or two about racing from my two older brothers. A head start is important. I lean into it, making for a streamlined profile.

He catches up to me. "Hey, speedy."

"That's right. Eat my dust!"

It's a close race, and we come to the opposite shore and smoothly follow the curve of the lake back to a slow stop, meeting in the middle.

He puts his hands on his knees, catching his breath. "Too close to call."

"Oh, I call it. I won."

He barks out a laugh. "Probably did. I'm beat."

"Let's get you back to shore, old man."

He takes off suddenly, racing me back. I laugh and race to catch up.

≈

Gage

I had a great time with Skylar today. I didn't expect to have fun at Winterfest. I thought I'd do my part and leave. Actually, I can't remember the last time I had fun at all. It's her. She has a way of just letting go in the moment.

"Almost time for the royal coronation," she says. "Should I put in your name for King Frost?"

I repress a shudder at the thought. "God, no. Just the thought of a coronation and royal ball makes me want to puke. Let alone actually being in the royal court."

She laughs. "But it would be so funny to see you up there with a crown and scepter. Mr. Grumps crowned king."

I'm about to say something about her being crowned Queen Perky when we're interrupted by Mrs. Ellis. I swear this woman is into me. There's a name for when an older woman goes for a much younger man—cougar. That's what she is. Why else would she keep showing up when I'm around and ask me so many personal questions? I've never dated someone decades older before, and I don't plan to now. No offense to eightyish women.

"Hello, Gage," Mrs. Ellis says. "Are you volunteering today or just enjoying Winterfest?"

"We were just ice skating," Skylar answers for me, standing up straighter.

"I helped build booths earlier, ma'am," I say.

The sharp-eyed woman studies us each in turn and then purses her lips. "Skylar, one of our volunteers came down with food poisoning, so Levi would like your help setting up for the coronation. He specifically requested you, which I think is a good sign. Remember our talk, dear?"

I stiffen. Levi? Isn't that the mayor guy Mrs. Ellis was pushing on Skylar earlier?

Skylar's all concern. "Oh no! What was the food poisoning from? I hope it wasn't from one of the vendors here."

"Actually, it was Caleb Robinson who got sick, and he believes it was from his wife's first attempt at stuffed chicken breast since they're both sick. Sloane's better with cars than in the kitchen. Each person should follow their natural abilities, I say."

Mrs. Ellis waves over at Levi and points to Skylar. He smiles at Skylar, a warm welcoming smile. "Now that's a real man."

Skylar turns to me. "I'd better go. It's a big job setting up for the coronation. I'll see you at work on Monday, and try not to be so grumpy."

"I'll help."

"But I thought the whole idea of a royal coronation and ball made you want to puke," Skylar says.

Mrs. Ellis chuckles and pats my shoulder. "Each to their own best abilities. Skylar and Levi will take it from here."

Skylar hurries to the big red barn just across the way, smiling up at Levi and talking in her enthusiastic way.

I clench my teeth, a burning sensation in my gut. I'm not jealous. I have no claim on Skylar. Relationships are a messy complication to my orderly life. I don't need them; I don't want them. And definitely not with someone I work with.

Besides, Skylar is kinda nice and sweet. I like her too much to let her get hurt by getting involved with me. I'm sure my ex was right about me being the problem—too closed off for a relationship. Otherwise, why would she have ended up in therapy right after she broke up with me? She always seemed to want more from me than I could give, always asking for reassurance that I loved her. I guess I'm just not built that way.

"I think Levi is ready to settle down," Mrs. Ellis tells me in a conspiratorial tone. "Just needed a little encouragement."

"Excuse me," I say and half jog, half walk over to the barn just as Skylar and Levi disappear into the storage area.

I swear I hear a cackle behind me. Almost sounded like an evil witch. My mind's playing tricks on me.

Skylar appears from the storage area, carrying a large plastic container. I'm so relieved to see her by herself and not lip-locked with Levi, I say the first thing that comes to mind. "You don't want to settle down with Levi."

Her brows shoot up. "What're you talking about?"

Heat rises from my neck to my jaw. "He's got too many responsibilities, being mayor and stuff. Then you'd have to be, like, Mrs. Mayor or something and—"

"Mrs. Mayor?" she asks like I'm crazy.

I feel crazy. All I know is that she shouldn't be with Levi, and as long as I'm here, he can't make a move. "Each person to their own best abilities, right? You decorate. I'll carry the heavy stuff with Levi."

She smiles sweetly at me, and my gut tightens in that way that tells me lust is building again. Not that it ever went away. I can control it. "Thanks, Gage. I had no idea you could be so helpful. Normally, you're just a big stone wall of no."

I carry the box over to a table for her. "It's Saturday. I'm off duty. You think Mrs. Ellis is hitting on me?"

She bursts out laughing. "Yes, Gage. I'm sure that's what's going on here." She pats my shoulder before pulling strings of white lights from the box. "I had no idea you were so funny."

I had no idea I could be jealous. What the hell is happening to me? I barely recognize myself.

I stride back to the storage area, where a surprised Levi looks over from behind a large red velvet throne. He's young for a mayor, thirty at the most, about my height, wide in the shoulders. I could take him.

"You're not Skylar," he says, amusement lighting his brown eyes.

I cross my arms. "I'm helping carry stuff. She's putting up decorations."

"That works. Grab that throne over to your left while I haul this one in."

I go for the throne, which is heavier than it looks, and head out, saying over my shoulder, "Skylar is chaos personified. Believe me, you don't want that in your life."

"She's a sweetheart from what I can tell."

I drop the throne with a thud and turn to him. "No."

He cocks his head. "No, what?"

"Just no."

His voice drops to a low calm tone that sets me on edge. "You gonna fight me for her?"

Think! What's the plan? Are you going to fight the mayor of Summerdale because he said Skylar is a sweetheart?

"She's in love with someone else," I say. It's the only thing I can think of that would keep an upstanding citizen like Mayor Levi away from her.

"Who?" he asks, challenge in his voice.

"Ace." That's my dog. I'm not used to lying, but I can't stop now.

"Is that a guy or a girl?"

I snort. "A guy." Then I carry the queen's throne out, dignity intact.

Besides, Skylar would never be happy with a straitlaced guy like that with all his duties and responsibilities. Not saying I'm the guy for her. Just not him.

8

Skylar

Omigod! I got roses for Valentine's Day! This is the most romantic thing that's ever happened to me. I've never had a Valentine's Day present ever, except for the cute paper hearts Mom used to make for us when we were little. Ooh! I hug the flowers to my chest, a bubbly light feeling filling me.

Could they be from Gage? We did have a nice time at Winterfest a few weeks back, and he's been warmer toward me at work. Not super reasonable, but also not stone cold. He takes the time to listen to me now and explain his side of things. Still doesn't budge much, but whatever. It's a much more pleasant work environment.

Well, it's not exactly *pleasant*. It's not awful either; it's just *charged*. Like a sizzling tension between us. I know he feels it too. I can see it in his eyes—primal heat. Is it possible he wants to take it to the next romantic level? I flush, my pulse racing. Do I want to get involved with him? The idea excites me.

On the other hand, what if things went south and he bad-mouthed me to our client? I need Spencer and Paige's good recommendation to pick up future clients. Would Gage do that? I'm having trouble trusting my instincts ever since I got burned by my former boss and her sleazy husband.

I breathe in the sweet scent of roses and look for the card tucked in the bouquet. Nothing here. Maybe it's in the box. I fill a vase with water and set the flowers in there, arranging them a little to show off the blooms. I smile to myself, imagining what Gage would write on the card, probably something short and sweet. I search through the box the flowers came in and all around the outside of it too. No card.

My smile drops as my mind flashes to the one man I don't want these flowers to be from—Brett, my ex-boss's husband. He's the reason my former boss has ruined my rep, and I can't get work in the wealthy area I used to work in not far from here. A sour feeling turns my stomach. I collapse the box for recycling with trembling hands. No, they're not from him. They have to be from Gage in a romantic gesture before my job ends with him. Right? It would be okay to get involved now that I'm done working at the restaurant. Today's my last day. Although, I still do have the job on Spencer and Paige's house in six weeks. Gage has to finish the home renovation there first.

I press a hand to my temple, feeling slightly crazed with all the back-and-forth, but it's important I stop and think things through. I tend to get excited and act impulsively, and I need to be more deliberate. I still have more work with Gage ahead, so that means, even if these lovely roses are from him, I need to keep professional boundaries. It doesn't matter how charged the air is between us, or that he gifts me with warm smiles sometimes. What matters is that I keep my professional reputation above reproach.

Actually, these roses could be from Levi. Mrs. Ellis has been pushing us together a lot. Levi, Gage, or a man I don't want in my life? Only one way to find out.

I bundle into my hand-knit wool hat, jacket, and boots, and make the short trip to Spencer's, the restaurant at the end of Lovers' Lane. What a cool name for a street, right? It's where Brooke and Max got together and now live, happily married, and Paige and Spencer too.

A few minutes later, I let myself into Spencer's with my

key and take a moment to admire the gorgeous front reception area. *I did this*. Okay, Gage built it, but I made it come to life. It's rustic—mostly wood and wrought iron—with a fireplace that makes it a welcoming space. To my left there's a separate room for the bar with a gorgeous antique mirror hanging in back. The bar is all glossy dark wood with glass shelves displaying the liquor bottles. Black leather swivel bar chairs with full backs line the bar to encourage lingering.

It's nice and warm in here. I take off my coat and hat, pushing my hat into the sleeve so I won't forget it, and step through to the large open dining room with floor-to-ceiling windows. The tables are in place now—more glossy dark wood with cushioned chairs. Frosted glass sconces on the walls give off a soft glow at night. In the day, the space is filled with natural light from the windows and the skylights. Spencer wanted the outside and inside to merge, and I think we've accomplished that. I hear some noise in the kitchen area to my right.

I push through the swinging door and find Gage and Spencer back there with a man I don't recognize.

I wiggle my fingers at them. "Gage, do you have a minute?"

Spencer jerks his chin at him. "Go ahead, Williams. I got this."

Gage looks back to the stranger and blows out a breath like he's annoyed by the interruption. "This won't take long."

My hackles rise. Why does Gage sound like I'm just an annoyance? I turn and walk into the dining room to wait for him, my happy feeling from before fizzling out. If he did give me these roses and still acts like an interruption from me is an annoyance, then he's not the man for me.

His gaze quickly takes me in from head to toe, from my hair—down today—to my red and white polka-dotted dress and knee-high black boots. I wore red for Valentine's Day, of course. He always checks out my outfit, though I get the feeling he thinks he's being subtle with how quickly he does it.

"What's up?" he asks. "I've got the building inspector here to clear the kitchen work."

I step closer and decide to give him the benefit of the doubt. He might not be the most expressive man in the world, but it's possible he was trying to tell me something with that gorgeous bouquet. Maybe, at some point in the future, there could be a chance for us. I'm breathless at the thought. I just can't let go of my romantic nature. It's hard to be cool and professional when I've got so much enthusiasm for life.

"I got the roses," I say.

"What roses?"

My stomach drops. If it wasn't him, then it was from someone I'm not interested in. I'll either have to reject Levi or make a quick exit from Max's place because Brett knows where I live. A chill runs down my spine.

"Who sent you roses?" he asks, his attention suddenly focused all on me.

I flush. I don't usually get his undivided attention. "Never mind." I turn to go, and he puts a hand on my arm, halting me.

I turn back. "Yes?"

"Why is someone sending you roses?"

My lips form a flat line. "It's Valentine's Day. It happens for some women." *Get the guidebook, please!* I really need to write *The Nitwit's Guide to Women*. There must be a huge market for it.

At his continued staring, I add, "Guys send roses to indicate their admiration. Not that you would know anything about that."

His lips twitch, his dark eyes sparkling with amusement, but then he frowns. "Who's sending you roses?"

I lift one shoulder in a careless shrug. "I don't know. There wasn't any card. I thought you might've been trying to, you know, be nice or something." I can't bring myself to say "romantic." I'm afraid he'll bust a gut laughing.

"By making a move on you?"

My cheeks flame, and I stare at a point over his shoulder, embarrassed at my assumption. So he's *not* making a move on me. *Fine*. That just makes everything simpler. When I see him in six weeks at Spencer and Paige's house, I'll pretend this whole embarrassing incident never happened. I must've been imagining the tension between us had veered into anything more than irritation.

I hold out my hand to shake. "Well, I guess this is good-bye. I won't be back to work on the house until late March if everything stays on schedule with the renovations, which I'm sure it will under your iron hand."

He stares at my hand and makes no move to shake it. "Did you line up a job in between?"

I purse my lips. "Can't even shake my hand, huh?"

"Do you have a job after Spencer and Paige's house?"

I shove my hand in the sleeve of my jacket and come up short, blocked by my stupid hat. Gage gently tugs the sleeve off me, looks inside, and pulls out my hat, placing it on my head. Our eyes meet up close, his suddenly warmer, like he cares about me. I'm so confused. The man gives off so many mixed signals. I wish I didn't like him so much. I admit it. Mr. Grumps grew on me, and I had a little hope for something romantic.

He helps me put my jacket on, holding it out for me to put my arms in the sleeves and settling it around my shoulders. The brush of his warm hand on the back of my neck surprises me as he sweeps my hair out of the collar of the jacket.

I turn to face him, my lips parting. "Thanks."

He searches my expression. "I bet Levi sent you those roses."

I keep my tone even. "Then I'll have to thank him." It's better than the alternative—unwanted attention from Brett at my home. No way I can stay there tonight or any time soon. I won't be able to sleep, worrying over every little sound. His interest in me didn't end in the break room, and I fear it's still going on.

Gage backs up a step. "I'd better get back to work."

"Right." I swivel on my heel and stride toward the door.

As soon as I step outside, my shoulders droop, my limbs heavy. So what if Gage doesn't think of me the way I secretly hoped? He made it a point to keep a professional distance from me, so it didn't make sense that he would send roses. Right? But my instincts drove me straight to him. I can't explain away the warmth he sometimes shows that makes me feel like the sun just came out and is shining all over me, or the rush of excitement I get when we're close. It scares me how wrong my instincts have steered me lately.

Who sent those roses? I shiver and head home to pack. It's time to make my next leap. I can't risk a run-in with Brett at my place, and I don't want to spill my guts to big brother. He'll interfere and make everything worse.

I pack up my stuff, trying to figure out how much I can get into my Toyota hatchback and how much I'll have to leave behind. It's not like I'll never come back to Max's studio apartment. I'll be back in six weeks. I texted a graphic designer friend who lives in Boston, and she said I'm welcome to crash at her apartment. I get the couch but whatever. It's better than waking at every sound, afraid I've got an unwelcome visitor. I let out a shaky breath. It's fine. Everything will work out.

It's dark by the time I make the final trip to my car. It's stuffed to the gills, and I can't see out the back window because of the piles of stuff. I only brought the necessities—clothes, shoes, toiletries, baking gear, aromatherapy diffuser, framed photos and art prints to keep me inspired. Also, my interior design studio, including art supplies, sample books of paints and fabrics, several portfolios, my laptop, and a few lamps for the proper lighting mood. What? An interior designer must have an inspiring space to create. I checked, and there's parking in my friend's neighborhood.

My brother Max believes I'm moving on to a job in the city before I return in six weeks. I just couldn't bear to have him send me more business articles or offer his wife's help again. I don't want him to see me as a failure, and I definitely don't want to share the shameful secret that's holding me back at the moment. I have to keep positive that things will improve soon. There has to be someone willing to take a chance on me.

I get into my car and plug my friend's address into the GPS. A truck idles at the end of the driveway, and I look up, expecting Max. My heart skips a beat. It's Gage. I really don't want to relive the embarrassing incident earlier when I so wrongly thought he gave me a romantic gift.

He powers down his window and stares at me. It's unnerving even from this distance.

I lower my window. "Hi."

He looks over my shoulder at the large pile of stuff behind me. "Moving out?"

"Yup. See you in six weeks." I wait for him to move on, but he doesn't.

Oh no. He's getting out of his truck.

I shrink down in my seat for no apparent reason. I'm a terrible liar, and the only reason Max accepted my excuse for leaving was because he was distracted by his dog Scout jumping on him in excitement. I really hope Gage doesn't ask too many probing questions. Like about my next job or my money situation or why I'm not staying put with my brother. My gut does a slow roll just thinking about all those problems piled up together.

Gage leans down to my window. "Where're you going with all this stuff?"

"Moving temporarily. I'll be back in six weeks."

"Where ya headed?"

"A friend's."

He stares at me for so long I flush hot and turn away. "Where's your friend live? Must be far if you're taking so much stuff."

I let out a breath of relief. He's just curious. "Well, you know, when you're an interior designer, it's important to keep your space inspiring."

He looks into the back seat and into the open trunk space of the hatchback. "Lamps, artwork, sketch boards, an area rug?"

"Mmm-hmm. Got to make my space cozy."

"You always redecorate a friend's space?"

"Well, she lives in Boston, so it won't be easy to come back for stuff I might want." A trickle of sweat beads down my chest.

He stares at me for a long moment, and I try not to fidget. "Skylar, I get the feeling you're not being entirely honest about your situation."

I gesture vaguely to all my stuff. "When you're a solo entrepreneur, it's one of the big perks—working from home."

"Okay, then you can work from my home," he says casually.

My mouth gapes, and he presses a finger under my jaw to close it.

His gaze is intense. "I'm hiring you to decorate my house. Boston to New Jersey is too far a commute, so you'll stay with me. I've got plenty of room for you and all your stuff."

I blink a few times in shock. Part of me is thrilled with the idea of a real project instead of spinning my wheels for six weeks on my friend's couch while I try to drum up business. But move in with him? Live with the sexy man I've been trying to keep a professional distance from, work on his house, and still remain professional?

Willpower can only go so far.

But didn't today's embarrassing roses incident cement the fact that he's not interested in me? Maybe at one point he was, but then it passed as he moved on to more important things, like his work. I bet he's perfectly content being a bachelor and making work the number one priority in his life.

Gah, it's so hard to think things through and ignore my natural instincts, which at the moment are screaming at me to drive straight to Boston and never look back. But Gage is offering a much-needed job.

He's also a complication I don't need.

"My friend's expecting me," I say. "And I have a lot of marketing work to do." I put on my cool professional look, but his brown eyes are warm again, and it makes me feel a little melty.

"You'd turn down a job in hand in the hopes of a future job?"

"It's complicated with…" I trail off. How do I explain I'm kinda into him and that makes things complicated?

He gives me his address and taps the top of my car as if it's all settled.

9

Gage

The moment the words were out of my mouth, I knew it's what needs to be done. Skylar's life is in chaos, and this is what I do, bring order to chaos. She *needs* me. I wait for her to catch up.

"Why do you need an interior designer?" she asks. "And, in particular, me."

I lean down into her car window to correct her. "I don't need you. You need me."

She stiffens.

"But it couldn't hurt to have you work your magic to help sell the place. I want to flip it and look for my next house to fix up."

A smile plays over her lips. She likes the compliment I worked in there. It's true, anyway, she's good at her job. "Oh, I remember now. You mentioned flipping your house a while back to one of the crew guys. He said it was an empty box."

"Basically."

She gets serious. "But are you sure you want me living and working in your house? Half the time we're fighting or having some kind of tense standoff over design issues."

"I'm sure. You've got no job lined up, are likely out of money or will be soon, and for whatever reason you don't feel comfortable staying with your brother. You don't have to tell me all the details. It's clear you have a problem, and I'm the solution."

"I don't need rescuing."

"No, you need a job, and we need to get going, or we're going to get stuck in monster traffic." I give her my address again, tell her to put it in her GPS, and head back to my truck.

"Has it occurred to you there could be an issue with two single people of the opposite sex living together?" she yells.

I bite back a smile and slowly turn. She wants me. I like knowing that, even if I don't plan to cross the line. The last thing I want is to dim that sunny sweetness. It's enough to have her nearby. Her cheeks are flushed red. I'm back at her car before I'm even aware of moving. "You'll have your own space. I told you I have plenty of room."

"Why would you make such a generous offer?"

To rescue you. I hold back saying that since she thinks she doesn't need rescuing. No reason to start our new project with a fight. "Do you always debate with your clients before letting them hire you? No wonder business is slow."

Her chin lifts, a pulse point in her throat beating wildly. I want to press my mouth to it. It's okay to have the impulse as long as I don't act on it. "This is a big deal, Gage."

"No, it's not. It's simple. You're making it more complicated than it needs to be."

She searches my expression, looking for signs that I'm going to make a move on her. I give her the hard expression I use at work when I don't want to deal with any interruptions. She's seen it enough.

"You're serious," she says. "It's just a job to you."

I still want her. I don't think it'll ever stop until I get her out of my system, but how can I do that and work with her? We've still got another project to get through at Spencer and Paige's house. I'm not a relationship guy, and it would get messy fast. This might be the stupidest move I've ever made, but my need to keep her safe trumps everything else. I can't have Skylar broke and struggling when I can give her a job and keep her safe from whatever is driving her from her brother's home. Maybe big brother is getting all up in her business and she's sick of it.

She nods once. "It's just a job to me too."

"Perfect."

She smiles slyly. "Turns out those roses were from Levi. Sweet of him."

My shoulders tense. What's that sly smile about? Is she trying to rile me up, or is she just secretly pleased he sent roses? She knows I don't think he'd be good for her.

"Guess you'll be Mrs. Mayor," I grumble.

"We'll see," she singsongs. "Back to business, I'll waive my design fee in exchange for a place to stay. You'll just need to pay my discounted wholesale cost for furniture and decorations."

My gut does a slow roll. I'm going to have to keep a tight rein on how much work she does at my place. I don't want to overspend on a house I'm just staging for a sale. In fact, I'd prefer it if she did nothing but live there. Maybe she could cook for me instead. Then I remember her awful healthy carrot-raisin cookies and decide I'm better off with takeout.

She offers her hand, the tips of her fingers brushing my stomach because I'm standing so close. My muscles jump, my pulse kicking harder. "Do we have a deal?"

"Sure." My voice sounds hoarse.

"How long do you think it'll take for the job?" she asks brightly like she's really looking forward to turning my place upside down.

She's got six weeks until her next job, so I leave it open-ended. "It might take a while. I only have furniture in two rooms."

Her eyes light up. "I can't wait to see it! I just knew if I leaped, the net would appear, and here it is. See, it's not always a bad thing to remain open to possibilities. I'll just text my friend about the change in plans and be on my way."

I'm alarmed at her sunny optimism in the face of her shaky situation. "No net, Miss Perky. It was me. Remember that."

She sucks in air.

"See ya at home."

"You're not my boss," she says. "You're my client. There's a difference."

I lean down to the window, and her cheeks flush. "Uh-huh."

"I mean it."

"Don't worry so much. Be open to possibilities." She scowls, not liking me quoting her. I tap the top of her car and stride back to my truck.

This was either the worst idea I've ever had or the perfect plan. Either way, I'm going to be in close quarters with the sexiest woman in Wonder Woman panties I've ever met. The only woman I've ever met in Wonder Woman panties.

Stop thinking about her panties!

≈

Skylar

I take one look at Gage's empty, soulless house and instantly know why he insisted I come here. He *needs* me. No one can live like this and feel good. And it definitely doesn't look welcoming enough for potential buyers. Is he just clueless about decorating, or does he find the starkness comforting? He does strike me as a guy not in touch with his softer side. He's all business all the time. I should be glad since I'm living with him. Makes things less complicated. So what if I moved him to my *wild dream* list?

Note to self: Stop adding Gage to lists.

The outside of his two-story house with white siding and black shutters is pristine with a neatly kept lawn and shrubbery, but the inside? *Shudder*. It's got good bones. An open floor plan with a modern kitchen with gray granite countertops and a matching island, white cabinets, and stainless steel appliances. The adjoining sit-in eating area is empty except for a hanging pendant light over where a kitchen table should go. Next to that is a large family room with a fireplace with the only furniture in the lower level—a large TV mounted on the wall above the fireplace, a black leather sofa, and a glass coffee table. That's it. No rug on the glossy hardwood floor. Plain white venetian blinds on the windows. Nothing on the white walls. There's an empty formal living room and office in the front of the house.

I imagine the only other room with furniture is his bedroom. I bet he has that metal frame that came for free with his mattress up there with a black nightstand. I'm not going to ask. There's plenty to do downstairs, and I don't want him to think that I'm super interested in checking out his bedroom, even if I am. This is a real job that he desperately needs me to tackle. And it will sure help my portfolio.

He returns from the glass patio doors off the dining area with Ace, his French bulldog. Ace is small and stocky, mostly white with black pointy ears and more black fur halfway to his muzzle, like he's wearing a black eye mask. He has a pushed-in flat nose that makes him snuffle a little. Gage heads for the sofa, and Ace follows him at a fast trot, the metal tag on his collar jingling. A moment later, Gage stretches out on the sofa and scoops Ace up with one hand, settling him on his chest. Ace licks his face and smiles at him. Gage smiles back, talking to him softly and scratching behind his ear. *Aww. Gage does have a heart!* Clearly he adores Ace, and Ace adores him right back.

"What do you think of the place?" Gage asks, not taking his eyes off Ace.

I cross to them, but there's no place to sit with Gage hogging all of the sofa. I perch on the arm of the sofa by his head. "It has enormous potential." *Because it's completely devoid of life.*

"Cool. No rush, though. Take your time getting settled in. You can take any of the empty bedrooms upstairs to make your own or the office downstairs. Order whatever furniture you like."

"Budget?"

"Don't go too crazy, but I've got money saved for this. Make sure it's stuff that would look good in another house too."

"Absolutely. I'll run purchases by you before I place the order." I stand. "I'll take a look around."

He finally looks at me upside down from his horizontal position. The angular lines of his face are striking. It'd be cool to paint his portrait. "Knock yourself out. I'm ordering Chinese. What do you like?"

"Surprise me."

He grunts in response. I have a feeling this will be a quiet household. Even his dog didn't bark when we came in, merely sat there looking at us expectantly. Gage told me he has a dog walker who takes Ace out twice a day, which helps keep him from going stir-crazy while Gage is at work. It says something about a person when they take such good care of their pet. I don't know why Mrs. Ellis called Gage a dud. He might be gruff and rigid, but he has a good heart.

I already saw the office downstairs, so I head upstairs. How empty are the bedrooms? I poke my head into the first one. Absolutely empty. White walls, beige carpet, a shuttered closet with only a rod. There's a plain white venetian blind on the single window. Next!

Unfortunately, he wasn't kidding when he said empty. The next two are the same empty starkness and plain palette. Guess I'll be sleeping on the floor.

I eye what must be the master bedroom at the end of the hall. Gage is still downstairs. Couldn't hurt to peek. I push the door open wider and take in a masculine space. A king-size bed with an iron sleigh-bed headboard and a fluffy white down comforter. Navy silk sheets and two matching navy silk-covered pillows. No throw pillows. A single wooden nightstand with a lamp. The inner sanctum has a minimalist look, but the silk and down blanket on the bed tell me he likes luxurious comfort close to his skin. Could rigid Gage be a secret sensualist? I sure am, though it's no secret. I even haul my aromatherapy diffuser from place to place just so I can indulge my senses.

What's Gage like after dark in the privacy of his bedroom?

I tear my gaze from the bed and step farther into the room, pushing open the door to a walk-in closet with hanging clothes, shelves, and drawers. The clothes only fill a third of the space. The en suite bathroom has a whirlpool tub, a glass shower, and double sinks. Everything is done in white—countertops, cabinets, and tile floor.

The house was probably built in the eighties. He invested in renovations on the place, bringing in a neutral color scheme, but clearly he had no clue where to start with decorating. I smile to myself. That's where I come in. He's lucky I was available.

I step into the bedroom and jump, my heart racing.

Gage is standing there, staring at me.

I put a hand to my heart. "Make a noise or something. You scared me."

He closes the distance between us, his dark eyes heated and locked on mine. I swallow hard. "What're you doing in here?"

I try for a smile, but my heart's still pounding, adrenaline racing through my system. "Just checking what might need my magic touch."

"Magic touch," he echoes, rubbing the back of his neck. "You can, uh, skip this room. No touching needed." He gestures vaguely around the room, a faint pink rising in his neck. "I mean no touching *the room*. Magic or otherwise." He blows out a breath. "You hungry? I hope so. I ordered Chinese. It's not here yet, but did you, uh, want a snack or something?"

Every nerve ending tingles. I'm not imagining this chemistry between us. This is the first time Gage has ever fumbled with words. It's because I'm standing in his bedroom. I'm glad to know it's not just me, even if I plan to keep our professional boundaries. I need this job, and I don't need messy complications that burn me in the end.

When he finally meets my eyes again, I smile and answer his question. "I'll wait for dinner, thanks. I'm going to bring in my stuff from the car now."

He turns abruptly and walks out the door, and I follow him down the hall, my heart slowing back to its normal mellow rate. I'm glad I lied and told Gage that Levi sent me those roses. The boundaries are so clear now. Actually, I asked Paige to check in with Levi for me in a casual way since she texts him regularly about officiating weddings. Not him. I guess it's good I don't have to reject Levi, but it only makes me more anxious about who did send them. I'm glad I'm somewhere no one knows about.

If Gage's house is my secret safe place, I guess that means I trust Gage. The fact that my heart goes crazy when he gets close can only be chalked up to lust and a fascination with a man so different from myself. I don't mind dealing with that in exchange for a safe zone and a cool new job. Sometimes it helps to always see the sunny side of life.

I meet up with Gage at the bottom of the stairs. "Eventually you'll want the upstairs done, right? Three of the bedrooms are so bland and empty."

"Nah, it's fine for me and Ace."

But I'm here too. Where exactly am I sleeping? My heart kicks harder as I think about that king-size bed. What if I ask and he just informs me I'll sleep in his bed the same way he informed me I'd be living here. The thought excites me way too much. *Wild dream! Not happening.*

I follow him to the family room and decide on a subtle approach to the sleeping situation. "I don't expect you to order a bed just because I'm here. I know it's temporary, but what will you do if you have guests?"

He pats the sofa, where Ace is curled up for a nap. Ace doesn't even blink at the disturbance. "This pulls out to a bed. That's where Livvie sleeps when she stays over."

A spike of jealousy hits me, and then I remember Livvie is his sister. Seriously, he wouldn't make his girlfriend sleep on the sofa. Does he have a girlfriend? That would be a whole different scenario. I can't ask. The earlier embarrassment over the roses he didn't send is still fresh in my mind.

"Where would you like to put your stuff?" he asks.

"Which bedroom has the best light?"

He tilts his head. "The back of the house is south facing, so I'd say the bedroom on the right." He gestures toward it.

"Perfect."

He heads out through the front door to get my stuff. I hurry ahead of him and open the hatchback.

He scoops up a few boxes. "Pile more on top."

I do, balancing stuff up to his chin. He strides back into the house. I pull my suitcases out and wheel them up the front walk.

I'm on my way out for a second trip for my stuff when I'm surprised by a couple standing on Gage's front porch.

There's a young woman with light brown shoulder-length hair and a guy with dark hair and a full beard and mustache. They're holding hands.

The woman smiles sweetly. "I'm Livvie. Who're you?"

"Hi. I'm Skylar."

"Are you moving into my brother's house?" she asks.

"Actually, I'm—"

Gage bounds out of the house. "Livvie, what're you doing here? You're supposed to be in school. What's going on?"

"Can we come in?" Livvie asks.

"Yeah, come in."

"I'll just get the rest of my stuff," I tell him and head back to the car.

I return with assorted art prints to find everyone standing awkwardly in the front hall.

"Help yourself to something to drink," Gage says gruffly to his guests and follows me upstairs.

I give him a quizzical look in the empty bedroom I claimed as an office. "Don't you want to be with your sister? I can get the rest of my stuff."

He runs a hand through his hair. "What if that guy, Charles…" He spits out the name with contempt. "…got her pregnant?"

My brows shoot up. "You're jumping way ahead here. Maybe she just wanted you to get to know her boyfriend better. Maybe they're serious."

"Serious," he echoes. "I just met him six weeks ago. How can they be serious already?"

"Just because you only met him recently doesn't mean she did."

His jaw clenches.

"Has she ever had a serious boyfriend before?"

"Just a guy in high school who joined the Marines. He was alright."

"Okay, so go talk to them."

He jolts into action, walking out the door and jogging downstairs ahead of me. Livvie and Charles are sitting on the kitchen island chairs with glasses of water in front of them.

"What's going on?" Gage barks as soon as he gets to the kitchen.

Oh my God. That's how he talks to his little sister?

Livvie gives him a small smile. "Gage, I have good news..." Her voice gets quieter at his hard expression, and I only catch the end of the sentence by the time I'm next to them. "...got engaged."

"No," Gage says.

Livvie's jaw drops. "What do you mean 'no'?"

"No. You're too young to be engaged."

"I'm twenty-one," she protests.

He jabs a hand at Charles. "I met this guy once. And now you're engaged? Are you pregnant?"

"No!"

"I love her," Charles says, putting a protective arm around Livvie. He looks at her with big puppy-dog eyes.

Aww! I totally believe him.

"No, you don't," Gage says. "You're both too young." He glares at Charles. "How old are you? Was this your idea? Where did you meet her anyway, some kind of drunken college party? I swear—"

"Gage, stop!" Livvie exclaims. "At least let him talk."

I give her an encouraging nod. That's the way to handle an alpha male with a 'tude.

Charles speaks calmly and confidently. "I'm twenty-one. The engagement was a mutual decision. We met at nursing school."

Gage scowls. "Two nurses. Both only twenty-one. Nope. Not happening. Charles, get out. Livvie, you stay. We need to talk."

I put a hand on Gage's bicep, and it's rock hard. A flutter low in my belly makes me drop my hand almost as soon as I make contact. He stills, staring down at me, his eyes flashing. Yup, he's riled up.

"Gage," I say gently, "maybe you could invite them to stay for dinner. Talk a bit."

"I'd like that," Livvie says quietly.

"Fine," Gage says, glaring at Charles.

"It's nice to meet your girlfriend," Livvie says. She turns to me. "You're the only one I've met besides Kate. So you're living here?"

Kate?

I put up both palms. "Oh, no, I'm not his girlfriend. And I'm not—"

"She's on the sleeper sofa," Gage says like that's the important thing.

My hands take on a life of their own, gesturing wildly as I explain my current situation. "I'm just here temporarily. I'm an interior designer, and Gage hired me to do design work for his house since he wants to stage it for a sale. It's an empty slate, so I have my work cut out for me."

Livvie gives her brother a pointed look. "I'll say. Good luck."

Gage turns to her, trying for a soft tone, but it still sounds rough. "You're always welcome here, Liv. My home is your home too; even if I move to my next fixer-upper, it'll still be near you."

"I know," she says softly.

If this is her home, there's no room that feels like hers. Then I remember he said she sleeps on the sofa when she's here.

Gage resumes glaring at Charles, seeming to be waiting for him to leave or maybe disappear in a puff of smoke under the power of Gage's burning eyes.

"Livvie speaks the world about you," Charles says.

Gage growls something unintelligible, stalks into the family room, and pulls his phone out, ordering more food.

Charles speaks softly to Livvie, reassuring her nothing will keep them apart.

"Congratulations," I tell the happy couple. "An engagement on Valentine's Day is extra romantic. You'll always get to celebrate this special time every Valentine's Day."

It occurs to me that Charles and Livvie could be enjoying a romantic Valentine's Day; instead they rushed here to share their happy news with a snarling dragon of a man. I feel bad for them, but at the same time Gage's reaction indicates the depth of his love and concern for his sister. He's a good guy. My own older brothers are better at using their words and naturally affectionate, so it's fascinating to watch Gage in action, in a car wreck kind of way.

"Can you talk reason to my brother?" Livvie asks me. "He's not taking this well."

Crap. If I'm her only hope, this is a very sad state. Gage rarely listens to me. "I'll try."

I turn, but he's not in the family room. I find him in the empty formal living room in the front of the house, staring out the front window. "How'd you know what to order for them for dinner?"

He stares out at the dark front yard. "Livvie always wants the same thing."

"And Charles?"

"Don't."

"Don't what?"

"Don't get in the middle of this." He walks to the front hall and paces like a caged lion. He wants to roar, and I can't let that be at his sister, who only wants to share her news with the brother she loves.

I follow him.

"What?" he snaps.

I hold my palms up. "Nothing. Seems like this is a surprise for you. Anything I can do?"

"You can tell her to go back to school. This isn't her break."

"How far away is her school?"

"About half an hour from here."

I close my eyes, reaching for patience. It's not like she drove cross-country with her big news. She can easily go back to school any time and not miss a thing.

"Gage, that's really not far."

He exhales sharply, his hands on his hips. "It's the principle of the thing. She should be so focused on school that she never thinks of leaving until her work is complete."

"Can we go with the assumption that she's completed all of her assignments, is super prepared for her next exam, and just came home to share her good news?"

"Good news," he grumbles under his breath.

"If you rain on her parade, she'll stop showing you her parades."

He stops and stares at me. "What parade, exactly?"

I lift my palms. "Her happiness. She's happy."

He frowns. "She doesn't know what she's doing. It's up to me to look out for her."

My own older brothers have always been there for me, but I never felt like either of them were father figures. "You seem more like her dad than her brother."

"In the ways that count, I am."

"How old are you?"

"Twenty-eight. Why?"

"You're seven years older and acting like her dad. What happened to your dad? Was he not around?"

He clamps his mouth shut.

"I get that. My dad left when I was four. I was lucky I had my grandfather around for most of my childhood plus my two older brothers."

"I'm all she has. Our parents bailed on us long ago."

I'm curious what exactly happened that made Gage take over with Livvie, but I keep my mouth shut. He's upset, Livvie's upset, and poor Charles is dealing with a hostile future brother-in-law. I'm about to suggest we go on a walk to cool off when he suddenly strides back toward the family room.

I follow at a slower pace. Maybe I should just butt out, get the rest of my stuff from my car, and set up my temporary office space. This is a family matter.

On the other hand, I can't stand to see a happy couple destroyed by Mr. Grumps. Maybe Gage has never been in love before and doesn't understand how powerful it can be. Of course, there was *Kate*. I'm so curious to know the situation with her.

I return to the family room to find the happy couple sitting on the sofa. Ace is curled up in Livvie's lap. Gage stands in front of the sofa, looking his usual formidable self as he glowers down at them.

I smile at them to make up for the glower. "First thing I'm going to do is order more seating for this room."

"Usually it's just me and Livvie," Gage says tightly, shooting Charles a dark look.

Livvie apologizes to Charles for her brother's rudeness.

Gage stiffens.

I attempt to lighten the mood, asking Gage in a teasing voice, "So you never have any women over?" Obviously a guy who gives off alpha pheromones like he does is never short of female company.

Livvie smiles. "None that I've seen in at least a year."

Gage gives us both a stern stare. "No comment."

I cover my shock with a smile. "Don't tell me you've been celibate for a year."

Livvie giggles. Gage's jaw sets in a hard line.

I turn to Livvie. "Is he always so rigid?"

She smiles. "Not always. He doesn't like to be caught off guard. Gage, I'm sorry to spring my big news on you, but it just happened, and the first thing I thought of was sharing the news with you."

Ace jumps off the sofa and climbs up on Gage's leg, sensing he needs comfort. Gage crouches down to pet him. Seems he's not ready to talk about her news, so I jump in with another attempt at lowering the tension in the room.

"Wait until you see the transformation of this place. It's going to be amazing. Warm and inviting. By the way, Gage, after dinner we should go over some options for the family room."

Livvie gestures around the space. "I'd say he prefers minimal stuff, right, Gage?"

He stands to his full height and looks around. "Yup."

"Then what am I here for?" I ask.

Gage gives me a wry look like I should know.

Livvie whispers something to Charles, and they grin at each other. *No, it's not like that.*

I sit on her other side and lean close to ask Livvie, "Has Gage ever lived with a woman before?"

"Besides me? No. That's why I was so surprised he let you move in."

I waggle my brows comically. "I suspect he's trying to seduce me."

Gage makes a choking sound of protest. *Guess that answers that question definitively.* "I was just trying to—"

I cut him off before he can share the current disaster of my career. "To find his own unique way to happiness. I'm hoping my sunshine and rainbows will lift him out of his permanent funk."

I look up at him, and he cracks a smile. "Sunshine and rainbows," he echoes gruffly. "Very useful."

Livvie elbows me. "I think you'll be good for him."

10

Gage

The four of us are gathered around the kitchen island, eating dinner. Skylar, Livvie, and Charles have the three island chairs, and I'm standing across from them, trying to keep an eye on Livvie and Charles, but Skylar keeps distracting me with all her questions for Livvie. I guess it's not all bad because I found out Livvie and Charles have been seeing each other for a little over five months, and once they both confessed they were in love with each other, they immediately started planning a future together. I only met the guy once less than two months ago. Why did Livvie wait so long to let me know about him?

Maybe she wanted to wait to be sure it was serious. I do tend to come down hard on any guys sniffing around her. Someone has to look out for her. So they're in love. Doesn't change the fact that she's only twenty-one and still has to graduate nursing school.

"What do you do in your free time?" Skylar asks Charles.

He laughs. "Not much free time with school, but what I do have I spend with Livvie."

"What about before Livvie?" she presses. "Hobbies? Interests?"

"I play piano."

Livvie smiles proudly. "He was in the all-state concert band in high school. He's an amazing musician."

Charles gives Livvie another lovesick smile. There's no denying the sincerity. Dammit. I hate to be the bad guy here, but someone has to be sensible. They're too young to know what they're doing.

Skylar rests her chin on her hand, smiling at Charles. "What else?"

"I was an Eagle Scout. I enjoy camping and hiking. I've been telling Livvie we should go camping this summer. It's probably our last summer before we're working full time."

"Totally agree," Skylar says. "Do all the fun stuff while you've got time. Once you're working, you only get a measly two weeks off. I spent my summer after college building a school in Kenya. It was amazing. I'd love to go back."

I stare at her. I didn't know that. It occurs to me I don't know much about her beyond the fact that she's a perky ball of sunshine with a good eye for design. And she's kind, loves to have fun, but still works hard. Sexy as hell, but that's not my business. Just because I saw her Wonder Woman panties and she now lives with me. *Don't think about it.*

And, of course, we can't forget Levi, the bringer of Valentine's Day roses. I should set down the ground rules tonight— no male visitors while she's here. I don't want to see or hear anything hot and heavy between them. Seriously, the mayor? He's all duty and responsibility; Skylar's not like that. And he smiles too much.

Skylar sends me a mischievous look before saying to Livvie, "So-o-o, tell me all of Gage's dirty secrets."

I set my fork down, tension setting in my shoulders. "Enough. There's nothing to tell." I don't want Livvie sharing about our parents. It's not a secret—all a matter of public record—I just hate talking about it.

Livvie grins. "Gage is a total fanboy of Amy Parker."

"She's funny," I say.

Skylar laughs. "I didn't know you had a sense of humor."

"It's well hidden," Livvie says.

"Gimme a break," I say.

Skylar looks thoughtful. "Is it her character in *Under the Table*, sunny, dependable Penny, that you adore?"

"Yes!" Livvie exclaims with a laugh.

I wouldn't say *adore*. She's just really cool.

Skylar points two thumbs at herself. "Who does that sound like?"

"Nothing like you," I mumble, though I'm suddenly struck by the similarities. Did I turn Skylar into my fantasy girl Penny? Or is that my type? My mind boggles. I've never been with a woman like that before, mostly because I'm not smiley enough to attract them. *Unlike Levi.* He is *not* welcome here.

"Oh my God!" Livvie exclaims. "That's why he invited you to move in. You're his sunny Penny."

Skylar laughs. "I had no idea Gage had a soft spot for Penny. Now it all makes sense."

I rub the back of my neck, not bothering to explain. Why should I be embarrassed? Let's look at the facts. Sunshine and rainbows are fun on TV—it got me through a rough patch in my own chaotic life—but it's not helpful at all in the real world. That's why Skylar needs me. I'm not panting after her or whatever, like she's my dream fantasy girl. This is just a favor for her. Yeah, that's all it is.

I finish my dinner while Livvie and Skylar talk about weddings, and Skylar gives her advice based on the Christmas Eve wedding she recently decorated for. Livvie and Charles look at Skylar's pictures on her phone, seeming to be excited about them. Next thing you know, Livvie will want to hire Skylar to decorate for her wedding. That wouldn't be such a bad idea. In five years. *Minimum.*

I wait for everyone to finish eating before I put my foot down. "Livvie, you're too young to be engaged. I want you to wait until you graduate. You have a scholarship. Those don't come around every day, and if you have any kind of break from school, it goes away."

Livvie rolls her eyes. "I'm not leaving school, and I graduate in three months."

"Once you're married, your priorities will change. That's

why I'm saying wait until you graduate to get engaged, and
then if you're still serious about each other five years down
the line, you'll know it's the right decision." There. A
perfectly reasonable argument. And Skylar says I'm unreasonable. Ha.

I glance at Skylar, her jaw agape.

What?

She shakes her head.

"Gage, I'm already engaged." Livvie thrusts her hand in
the air, showing off a small diamond engagement ring. "You
expect me to break off the engagement for three months and
then get engaged and then wait five more years to get
married? Did I get that right?"

I'm glad she's getting it, though there's a bit of an edge to
her voice. "Yes."

Skylar's eyes bore into me with some message I ignore.
This isn't her business.

"What's wrong with being engaged before graduation?"
Charles asks.

I set my palms on the island and lean forward, giving him
my fiercest glare. "What's wrong is that it will make her lose
focus. Livvie can get engaged once she gets her degree."

"But we're not getting married until after graduation,"
Charles says. "We both want to finish our degrees first."

I have to give him credit for not folding under my glare.

"Yeah," Livvie says. "And even if we were getting married
right away, that's okay too. We're adults."

Very young adults stupid with love.

I try again with a reasonable argument. "It's too easy for
you to get distracted by wifely or even motherly duties.
That's why you need to wait five years after graduation to get
married."

"Wifely duties?" Livvie asks incredulously. "What do you
know about wifely duties?"

"I know what Mom was like. You have the same need to
take care of someone, and all I'm saying is take care of you
first."

Livvie's lips set in a firm line. "I'm not breaking my engagement."

"It's not the right time."

Livvie stands abruptly. "You're not my dad."

"I'm the closest thing you've got!"

"I came here to share my happy news, and all you did was make me feel like shit!"

I stare blankly at her. Livvie never gets upset with me. She's always smiling and agreeable. Never has she gone against my wishes. "Liv, I'm trying to help you."

Her cheeks flush red, her eyes flashing. "You don't know what you're talking about, all alone here in this empty house." She turns to Skylar. "Get out before he blocks out all those rainbows and sunshine you like." She tugs Charles's arm. "Let's go."

I watch in shock as my baby sister rushes for the door. Charles grabs their coats from the sofa, shoots me a dark look, and strides after her.

A soft hand lands on my arm. Skylar. "Don't let her leave like this," she whispers. "What if she elopes without telling you?"

That sets me into action. I race after them and catch Livvie just as she's stepping outside. "Don't you dare elope!"

Livvie and Charles look at me like I have two heads. Then he puts his arm around her and guides her down the front walk.

I turn back inside, dreading having to explain myself to Skylar, but she's not there. I walk back toward the kitchen to clean up and see her climbing the stairs.

"Where're you going?" I ask in a harsher tone than I mean to.

"I'm going to get settled upstairs and give you a chance to chill."

I suddenly want her around. I want to share my sordid family history and why it's so important Livvie starts her adult life with a stable foundation independent of any man. My chest aches fiercely, my muscles tight, wanting to straighten out Livvie and helpless to do so. She won't listen to me. This has never happened before.

It seems by protecting Livvie from the worst of our childhood, I only made things worse. Now she doesn't see how history is repeating itself. Mom never got her degree, dropping out to get married and have me. She was in no way prepared for life without Dad, and she paid dearly for it. I can't let Livvie end up like her.

∼

Skylar

I've been here a week now, and Gage and I have settled into a routine of sorts. He brings take-out dinner home for the two of us, and after dinner, I go over design plans. I've got the whole downstairs planned out and orders put in. Tonight when he gets home, I'm going to go over the upstairs with him. I managed to convince him Livvie needed a space to call hers (I didn't mention Charles, but I'm putting in a bed large enough for two), and it would be good to put at least a minimum into the other empty rooms for future guests. He can always take the furniture with him to the next house. I didn't say nieces or nephews, but that's probably the reality down the line. Livvie's still planning to get married after graduation, though they haven't set a date yet. Gage is still convinced he can reason with her before that happens. I'm hoping he'll see reason before he permanently pushes her away.

I'm on the sofa with my laptop, working on marketing efforts in any way I can, trying to track down potential clients and friends of friends. It's rough out there. I try to understand where my former boss is coming from—a hurt and wounded place, betrayed by her husband. It's the only way I can forgive her and move on with my life.

The interior door from the garage opens, and Gage appears in the kitchen with a take-out bag from a Thai place nearby. He sets it on the island counter.

I pop off the sofa at the same time as Ace sleeping on the pillow next to me, and we head over to greet him.

"Hello, roomie," I say.

He flashes a bright smile that warms me all over. I've been getting that smile every time he comes home from work and sees me, like he's happy I'm here. "Sky." I love that he uses my nickname now.

My pulse thrums through my veins as he approaches. And then something surprising happens, he stops only a breath away, his hand lifting as he gazes into my eyes. His gaze trails to my cheek, landing on my lips. Is he going to hug me? Kiss me? I'm breathless with anticipation.

He shakes his head, taking a step back. "I brought Thai." His voice sounds hoarse.

"I saw that," I chirp. I take a deep breath and smooth my palms down my jeans. "Let's eat."

"Good idea." He shifts to the island counter and empties the bag before informing me gravely, "I still haven't heard from Livvie."

He says this every night. She's not responding to his texts or calls. I get it. She's mad that he's not supportive of her engagement. I've tried gently explaining her perspective to him, but he refuses to acknowledge that she could be fine just as she is. Tonight I try a different tactic.

"You need to offer her an olive branch," I say, heading to the kitchen cabinet.

He starts opening containers. "I'm not agreeing she's doing the right thing. Can you get the plates?"

"One step ahead of you," I say, setting the plates down. I grab napkins and silverware too. I know where everything is, not that there's much. Just the basics.

"Renovations are coming along," he says. "Nearly done the master bath." He means at Spencer and Paige's house. My work starts when his is nearly complete.

"Excellent."

We settle at the island to eat in companionable silence. Well, he enjoys the silence while I spend my time envisioning the finished view from here with a fully outfitted dining area and family room. I've even got a cute red plaid dog bed with a fluffy Sherpa interior for Ace. He's a real cool dog, never excitable. Kinda reminded me of his owner until the recent Livvie upset.

"Like what?" Gage says out of the blue.

"Sorry, what're we talking about now?"

"Livvie," he says as if it's obvious.

Ah, the olive branch.

"Oh, well, I think it would be good to take them out to dinner. Somewhere in neutral territory, where it's harder for anyone to yell or walk out. You know, a civil conversation in a nice restaurant."

"With what's-his-name," he says in disgust.

"Charles is not the problem here. He seems like a good guy, and he's obviously in love with her. Did you see his big puppy-dog eyes every time he looks at her?"

Gage mutters something that sounds like *stupid*.

"There's nothing stupid about love."

"Have you been in love?"

"Yes, once."

"Why'd you break up with him?"

I smile because he assumed it would be me who ended it. Like no one would ever want to dump me. Or maybe I'm just reading into things. "We were heading in different directions after graduation. That's all."

He points at me. "See? Too young. That's what I keep trying to explain to Livvie. What's the rush? She's only twenty-one."

"Love doesn't work on a convenient schedule."

He grunts, which I've learned means he's listening.

"They seem very compatible. Professionally too. Their work schedules could mesh nicely, they'd both understand the stresses of the workplace, and they're also both nurturing, caring people. Honestly, I don't see the problem."

He stands abruptly, clearing his dishes. "You wouldn't."

"Why, because I don't have a problem with someone's happiness?"

"Because you only see the good side of life."

I set my fork down, my appetite gone. "That's not true." *That's Skylar for you, free spirit, not a care in the world.* My whole life my family saw me that way, and it stopped them from seeing I'm more than that. I have deep feelings and, yes, joy in life, but also substance and a work ethic.

"Name one bad thing that's ever happened to you," he says in a challenging tone.

I stand stiffly, my temper barely controlled. "I don't have to explain myself to you, but my life hasn't always been sunshine, still isn't, but I choose to look at things in a positive light as much as humanly possible."

He shakes his head and puts his dishes in the dishwasher.

I toss the take-out containers in the trash in the garage. When I return, he's at the kitchen sink, his hands on the counter, his head bowed.

My heart lurches. It's so sad how clueless he is about Livvie. Clearly he loves her, but he's going about this all wrong. It tortures him that she won't talk to him.

"Gage, just invite her and Charles to dinner. I'll go too, and we'll call it a double date. It'll take the pressure off. As long as you don't insist they break their engagement, I think she'll warm up to you again. And I could talk to her about what she'd like for a bedroom just for her. That way she'll feel like she has a home here. You can take her setup with you to your next place too."

He slowly turns, his voice gruff. "You'd do that for me?"

"Of course!"

He studies me for a moment. "What would Levi think about you going on a double date with another guy?"

I flush with guilt. Gage informed me I couldn't have Levi over, believing I'd actually want him here after he sent me roses for Valentine's Day, which, of course, he didn't do. This is why I hate lying. One builds on the other until you can't stop. It's how things got away from me when I claimed I found a leprechaun as a kid. Hey, I learned early it's better to be honest. In retrospect, no one in my family believed me, but they did a convincing job of egging me on until I cracked under the pressure and confessed all.

This is the last lie, I swear!

"I told Levi we should just be friends." Actually, I haven't seen or talked to Levi since Winterfest about a month ago.

"Why?"

I shrug. "Just wasn't feeling it. No chemistry, I guess."

He grunts, a pleased-sounding grunt. "So you don't mind pretending we're on a date? It wouldn't be, uh, I dunno, difficult?"

I grin. "Because you're difficult? No-o-o. Say it's not true. You're just as easygoing and sweet as can be."

He gets serious. "You don't have to. It's a huge favor, and you owe me nothing. I—"

"It's fine! I was just teasing. Besides, I want you and Livvie to make up. She obviously means the world to you."

He blinks a few times. "She's the only family I've got." His voice cracks.

I lift my hands, impulsively wanting to hug him, but not sure if it's appropriate. "Okay. Get in touch with her, and then after your shower, we'll talk about potential design plans." He always showers after dinner. In any case, I've learned it's better to call things "potential" so he doesn't immediately dig his heels in. Gage doesn't respond well to change or surprises, which explains a lot about our earlier work relationship. I'm used to going with the flow. Maybe we should call Livvie's engagement a "potential marriage" instead. Ha!

I go upstairs to my bedroom studio to set up my ideas to show him. First thing is to warm up his bedroom space while still keeping it soothing for sleep. Then a room for Livvie and a room done in a gender-neutral yellow color that could be a kids' bedroom. Just a simple daybed and nightstand for the room I work in, staged as a guest room or a place to curl up with a book. Not that I've ever seen Gage reading. Mostly he watches sports and hangs with Ace.

"Sky."

I startle from my spot sitting cross-legged on the floor. I was so engrossed in my work I didn't notice Gage approach. He leans against the doorframe, one hand resting on the side of it. His hair is damp from the shower and slicked back, the hard angles of his face more pronounced. My mouth goes dry. He's in a blue thermal Henley that stretches across his wide chest, hugging the swell of his shoulders and biceps, sleeves pushed up to reveal those sinewy inked forearms. Jeans and bare feet. Gage in a suit was tempting, but Gage relaxed after a shower is sexy as hell. It's getting harder to resist him by the day.

"Yes?" I ask in a throaty voice.

"She agreed to a double date if I give Charles a chance, so thanks. That was a good move."

I smile. "You're welcome."

He smiles back, his eyes warm, all the hard lines of his face softening. Breathtaking. He's breathtaking. "Not this weekend, the one after that. Is that good for you?"

"I'm wide open."

"Great!" He gifts me with another smile.

"You should smile more. Good look for you."

His neck pinkens. "Yeah?"

"Yeah," I say softly.

He smacks the doorframe overhead. "I have a poker table and chairs in the basement. I'll put them in here so you don't have to work on the floor."

"I don't mind." *Don't go.*

"It's done. Be right back."

I gather my materials and laptop and set them to the side to make room for the new stuff.

After he sets the table in the corner of the space with two chairs, he turns to me, studying me in that quick way he thinks is subtle from the top of my head to my toes. I'm in a peach floral top with black jeans and ankle boots today. This time his gaze lingers, warming me. First on my hips, up my body, pausing on my lips and, finally, my eyes.

My lips curve up. "You know women can tell when they're being checked out."

"I wasn't checking you out."

"What were you doing?"

"Nothing."

I give him the same thorough once-over, lingering on the

wide expanse of chest stretching the shirt to his corded inked forearms. I don't go below the waist because I'm not rude. Though I know exactly how his jeans hug that fine ass. Ha.

He chuckles. "Point taken."

He turns to take a seat on the other side of the table, and I admire his ass. This is an important step forward in our collaboration—mutual admiration society. Nothing wrong with that. Except he smells so fresh and clean I want to lick him all over.

He smiles at me, and my heart kicks harder. "So what do you have planned, brilliant woman?"

I get my laptop and take the seat across from him. "Oh, I like that. And why am I brilliant?"

"You solved the Livvie problem."

I put a hand to my heart modestly. "I can't take all the credit. She must've wanted to reconcile."

"You took the pressure off with the double-date idea. I owe you."

I shake my head. "No way. If anything, I owe you for letting me be your roomie and giving me such a great project."

He looks at me intently, his voice gruff. "We should get you a bed to sleep in."

I open my laptop, suddenly flushed with heat. "I actually had a daybed in mind that can double as a love seat for a cozy reading area."

"Whoa, a love seat. Let's not get too personal here."

I check his expression. His eyes dance with amusement. He's actually joking with me! "We'll call it a friendship seat."

"Fair enough."

"It'll be good to make the home feel more lived in. When you put it on the market, it makes it easier for people to imagine themselves here."

He leans back in his chair. "Yeah. I should start looking for a new place close by Livvie's school."

"Gage," I say gently, "you do know she might not stay in the area. She could move to wherever her new job is or where her husband's new job is."

His jaw clenches. "My job is to stay put so she has a home to come back to."

My heart squeezes. I want to stroke the tension from his jaw, soothe him and tell him he's done his job where Livvie's concerned, and everything will be okay. But it's not my place. He's my client, not my boyfriend.

"Now show me your plans so I can make sure you're not turning this place into a fun house," he says.

"Oh, no, never fun."

"You know what I mean."

I go over the plans, showing him the 3D rendering on my laptop as well as color samples for walls, floors, and curtains. I also have some furniture ideas. He mostly just listens, no questions asked, until we get to his bedroom.

"Nothing for mine. It's got everything I need."

"It has two things. A bed and a nightstand."

"That's all I need."

"Well, your potential buyers could be a married couple. It would help them to feel at home if you at least add a second nightstand."

"How hard is it to imagine a second nightstand?"

I let out a breath. "Say you take all this stuff to your next place and you get a wife. Maybe she'd like to feel at home with a dresser and a nightstand of her own."

"I'm not getting a wife."

I sit straighter. "Oh." Good to know, and also sad. *So* sad. For him, I mean.

I press on. "Okay, what about curtains? Or art?" At his frown, I narrow it down even more sparsely. "How about just an area rug to warm up the space? Then when you wake up on a cold winter's morning, your bare feet will touch a warm soft rug instead of cold hardwood floor."

He stares at me for so long I don't think he's going to answer until he finally says, "Okay, one rug."

I smile. "And how about a framed picture of you and Livvie? Wouldn't that be nice?"

"Yes, but not in the bedroom. You can put that on the mantel in the family room."

"Do you have any pictures I could use?"

"Sure." He walks out and heads to his room, so I follow. He disappears into the walk-in closet, reaches for the high shelf, and brings down three photo albums. "Livvie put these together for us."

I take them and sit on the end of his bed. He joins me. The first album is when they're young but not babies. Gage looks about nine, and Livvie is two. I see a young woman who looks tragically sad in the background. "Is that your mom?"

"Yeah."

"She looks so sad."

"She was. She lost everything she cared about when Dad left."

But she still had her kids! My chest aches with sadness—for her and for Gage and Livvie. I flip to the next page. Most photos are of the two kids with only a few of the three of them together. Clearly, Mom was the photographer except for the occasional birthday when someone else must've taken the picture to include her with the kids. Even when she's smiling, she looks sad.

I turn to him. "Are your baby pictures in one of these albums? I bet you were a fierce-looking baby."

He doesn't laugh. "Livvie didn't want any pictures with Dad in them, and I don't blame her."

"How old were you when your dad left?"

"Nine. He didn't leave voluntarily." He glances at me and then stares at the photo album. "He's in jail."

I suck in air.

He stares straight ahead. "Yeah, most people have that reaction."

"Gage, I'm so sorry."

He jerks his chin. "He deserved it. He played fast and loose with other people's money and then lost it all. All of his assets were seized, and he went to jail for fraud and a slew of other charges. He crossed a lot of lines he never should've crossed. Mom never recovered. She loved him and the life-style equally. We went from wealthy to poor overnight. She had a breakdown when I was in middle school and was institutionalized for a month. I took care of Livvie as best I could in our little apartment."

I squeeze his arm. "She was lucky to have you."

He exhales sharply. "Thanks. Mom came back, but was never what you'd call stable. She drank too much, dabbled in drugs, occasionally left for weeks. Once Livvie went to college, Mom abandoned our apartment and moved in with her drug dealer. Easier to stay high than deal with life. I tried to get her help, tried to get her out of there, but she fought me and told me she never wanted to see me again. Livvie stayed far away from her too after that."

"That's terrible. You must be so strong to come out of that environment as capable and successful as you are."

His brows shoot up. "That's how you see me after everything I just told you?"

"Absolutely."

He stares straight ahead. "Some people say my family is trash."

"They're wrong. You and Livvie are good people, and your mom probably has some mental health issues. She needs help. That doesn't make her trash. I'd like to think your dad learned his lesson the hard way and has reformed."

He shakes his head. "Sunny optimism strikes again."

"It helps to give people the benefit of the doubt. It also helps to find a way to forgive them."

He lifts his palms. "So that's my life. Chaos. All I ever wanted was to provide a stable foundation for Livvie. I helped her apply for scholarships and financial aid so she could go to college for nursing. She got into a good school too. You see why it's so important for her to finish? How can she have a stable life as an adult without her education and a good job? I don't want her to be dependent on a man like our mom was, because that can go away. I can't stand to think of Livvie falling apart like that."

"She won't because she had you as an example."

"You don't know that for sure."

"I have a good feeling."

"Feeling," he grumbles.

I elbow him. "That is the most you've ever said to me, and I understand you so much better now."

He stares at the photo album. "Yeah, well, I didn't want you to think I was a monster when it came to Livvie. Look at her here trying to hula-hoop in the apartment courtyard with the big kids. She's so little and innocent."

I turn the pages, looking for the perfect picture of the two of them. "This one. I can have it enlarged and frame it." Gage and Livvie are outside. Livvie is on a bike with pink handle-bars, and Gage is standing proudly next to her.

"Big moment," he says, smiling at the picture. "She'd just learned to ride at ten years old. It took forever. She was so uncoordinated, mostly because she was afraid, but I coached her through it. I knew she could do it."

"How did you get past her fear?"

"Little by little, day in, day out until she trusted me abso-lutely to guide her."

"Even after a fall?"

"Especially after a fall. I'm the one who puts things right."

He sounds so sweet and caring in that moment that I impulsively wrap an arm around his waist and give him a squeeze. Our gazes collide. His eyes darken as his gaze drops to my lips.

"You actually are sweet," I whisper.

"You're the sweet one." His hand comes up to cradle my jaw, his thumb brushing across the sensitive skin under my ear. My heart pounds against my rib cage as his eyes search mine.

"Yes," I say, though he didn't ask a question out loud.

His lips meet mine, not too hard, not too soft. It's a perfect kiss, and the moment he pulls away, I want more.

I thread my fingers through the hair at the nape of his neck and bring him back for another. And another. Each kiss leaves me hungry for more. I taste him, and he groans, his kiss suddenly ravenous. Raw lust like I've never felt before rushes through me, a low ache reminding me just how long it's been.

I throw my arms around his neck, giving myself over to

passion as the spark that was always there turns into a bonfire. And then he's lowering me under him, and I sink into soft comforter, covered by hard man. Everywhere I touch, he's all hard muscles and planes. I slide my hands under his shirt, reveling in all that heated skin.

He kisses along my neck, his scruff rubbing against the sensitive skin, sending electric sparks down every nerve.

He lifts his head. "So sexy," he says in a low grumble that I suddenly realize is just how he talks, not an indicator of grumpiness. I don't think I'll ever call him Mr. Grumps again after this.

I grab his head and pull him back to me, kissing him passionately. His fingers delve into my hair, his tongue spearing into my mouth. My insides coil tight and hot.

He breaks the kiss. "I shouldn't…we…this is too weird—"

I shake my head vigorously. "Not weird at all. It would be weird if you stopped."

He pulls my arms from his neck and eases off me, standing next to the bed. "This was my fault." He stares at my mouth, which still tingles from his kisses. "It won't happen again."

I prop up on my elbows. "What if I want it to?"

11

Gage

I take in her lush lips, the bright shine of her blue eyes, the faint beard burn on her neck and force my hands to stay by my sides. "Sky, this was a mistake. I've got walls. Those walls have walls. The only one who ever gets past them is my sister. You don't want to get involved with me, you'll only end up hurt."

"Tell me about your walls."

"No."

"Does this have something to do with Kate?"

I wait for the cold burn in my gut at her name, but there's just a guilty twinge.

She pats the mattress next to her. "Sit."

"Not a good idea."

"I'm not seducing you. I'm getting to know you better. It's called intimacy." She flops backwards on the bed, her feet still flat on the floor, and pats the space next to her again. "You share one thing, and I'll share one thing."

Who could resist the invitation?

I sit on the edge of the bed and flop backward, imitating her. The mattress bounces, and she laughs, taking my hand in hers and entwining our fingers together.

"What's your Kate baggage?" she asks.

I stare at the ceiling. "I hurt her, not intentionally, but I guess just by being me."

She squeezes my hand. "How long were you together? Who broke up with who? And what lie did she tell you?"

"That's a lot of questions."

"Because you're slow on the details."

"I was working on her house, things ended badly, and I still had a month to go with that godawful tension. You see the parallels here?"

"Yes, of course."

"Then why're you still holding my hand?"

She turns her head and smiles at me. "Because I like you."

Warmth replaces the cold in my gut, the tension leaving me. I look at the ceiling again. "You won't like me much after you hear."

"I'll be the judge of that."

"We were together three months; she ended it and said the reason she had to break up with me was because I was so closed off she had to go to therapy."

She jackknifes upright. "Bullshit! I can't believe she put that on you, especially with your mom's mental health issues. You told her about your family, right?"

I sit up. "Well, yeah."

Her lips form a flat line. "She had no right to put that on you."

"Sky, she always wanted more from me than I could give, always wanted reassurance that I loved her. Obviously, I'm too closed off if she couldn't even tell I cared about her. She was the first serious relationship I had."

"Maybe she needed therapy. Maybe no one could've given her enough because she needed to make herself happy first. She sounds like a terribly insecure, vengeful woman. Knowing your mom's history, it was cruel of her to blame you for her own issues. I want to shake her, and I'm a pacifist!"

My lips curve up. "You sure fought with me a lot for a pacifist."

"Those were constructive arguments. I never clobbered you with my purse like I wanted to, now did I?"

"Your peaceful side really shines through."

She wraps her arms around my middle and gives me a sideways hug. I wrap an arm around her shoulders and give her a squeeze. I like that she leapt to my defense, but it doesn't change the fact that I'm a bad bet.

She pulls away, studying my expression. "Do you still blame yourself?"

"I just don't think I'm cut out for relationships, and I don't want to hurt you."

"I appreciate your honesty. Now I'll share one thing."

"Okay," I say slowly, curious what baggage Skylar could possibly have. She's always so sunny and enthusiastic, it's hard to imagine anything bad ever happened to her.

"Did I ever mention I grew up in a lake house on Lake Summerdale that my hippie grandfather helped build?"

"You did. Back when I was at your place before Spencer and Paige's wedding."

"You remember that from back then?" She scrunches her brows in deep thought. "That was almost two months ago."

"There's not much about you I don't notice or remember."

She beams her sunny smile at me, and my heart kicks harder. "It's nice to hear you say stuff like that."

"You're hard to miss when you're always in my face."

She shoves my shoulder, and I laugh.

"What about your lake house?" I ask.

She sighs. "I miss it a lot. Sometimes I imagine working my magic on it and giving it a modern makeover. It hadn't been updated in decades. So that's my secret fantasy."

I grin. "Not as racy as I hoped your secret fantasy might be. Do you have a picture of it?"

"Yeah, I took so many before it sold. Be right back."

"You don't have to show me now."

She stands. "I want to." Then she dashes out the bedroom door, taking all her warm energy with her.

I rub the uncomfortable ache in my chest. "I hope you're not running away!" I hate feeling vulnerable. I shared, dammit.

"Hang on!" she calls from down the hall.

"You're the one who's supposed to be an expert on intimacy! Whatever that means!" I flop back on the bed. This sharing stuff is exhausting, especially when nothing I say seems to put her off. How am I supposed to keep a safe distance when she's completely oblivious to all the danger signs I'm putting up?

I stare blankly at the ceiling. Is it possible I wasn't the reason Kate had to go to therapy? She said she'd never been before, but she needed it after me. Did she just say that because she didn't want to admit the real reason she needed therapy? Maybe she didn't even know why, but just lashed out in her misery. I've certainly seen that when Mom was in a bad spot.

The mattress shifts as Skylar returns and pokes me in the belly. "Hey!"

"Sit up. I want to show you my pictures."

I do, meeting her sparkling eyes. I never want to be the reason to make that inner joy of hers dim. She scoots close against my side and shows me her phone screen. I take the phone and scroll through several pictures of her lake house. It's a wood-sided ranch home with a large attic. A staircase on the side leads to a wooden deck on the back, facing the lake view. Plain, but I see the appeal right there on the lake.

I turn to her. "Do you ever drive by just to look at it?"

"I can't. The new owners demolished it and put up a shiny new two-story house. It's all weird boxy angles and glass." Her voice chokes, and my chest aches in sympathy. "I can barely stand to drive by it."

I rub her back. "Sorry to hear it."

She sniffles, takes her phone back, and scrolls through her pictures again, stopping on a fairyland mural painted on what must've been her bedroom wall. There's a canopy bed with sheer drapery too. "I think I miss this most of all."

"Maybe you could find the artist and have another mural painted."

"It was me."

My brows shoot up. "You did that?"

"Yeah, when I was ten."

"When you were ten!" I take her phone and enlarge the picture, studying it. "You are seriously talented. Do you have other paintings?"

"Just a few small ones I hang on the wall."

"How are you not painting all the time?"

"Because being an artist isn't a stable career choice. After Dad left, Mom struggled to pay the bills on her administrative assistant salary. He never sent child support. Anyway, Mom drilled it into my head that it was great to be creative, but I had to find a real career that let me use my creativity. Voila! Interior designer."

I stare at her for a long moment. "I hate to say it, but I agree with her. Still, it's hard to believe you never paint anymore."

"I'm trying to establish my solo business. You know, build my portfolio and find new work."

I nod. "Makes sense."

"Okay, now I shared, so it's your turn to share an intimate detail."

"I already shared."

She pokes my chest, and I grab her hand, holding it there. "So share again," she says. "Oh, your heart's pounding. This is really hard for you, isn't it?"

I drop her hand and look away. "You're starting to make me see the bright side of things. That could be dangerous."

She gets off the bed and faces me. "The real danger is hanging out on your bed with you."

I lift a hand toward her, wanting her back. "Hey, I'm not dangerous."

"I don't mean you're dangerous. It's us. I think we need to back it up here a bit for both of our sakes."

She turns and walks out the door.

"Us?" I say to the empty room.

You know when you've got a beautiful sexy woman living with you and you want to hook up with her, but instead you share a bunch of intimate stuff, and then suddenly you find yourself doing crazy things? Uh, me neither.

Which is why I'm *not* sitting in my car in the garage with a giant gift bag next to me on the seat. It's been three days since I shared about my dysfunctional family and my disaster of a relationship, and for reasons I can't comprehend, Skylar is even warmer and friendlier than before. I'm trying to enjoy it and not question her sanity. Anyway, I've been thinking a lot about her artistic talent, which is why I have this giant gift bag. I exhale sharply, heat creeping up my neck, and get out of the car. I should be able to walk into my own house.

I go in the door that leads to the kitchen, and Skylar appears, eyes bright, radiant and smiling. The tension drains from me. My nerves—gone. Sore muscles from a long slog of a day—gone. My limbs are light, heat radiating through my chest. I love seeing her when I come home every day.

"Sky." One word that's come to mean so much.

"Gage," she says with equal sincerity before bouncing on the balls of her feet. She's wearing a tiny white cropped cardigan over a pink dress that bounces with her movements. *God, she's beautiful.* "The new family room furniture arrived today. Wait until you see how it all came together! Oh! Is that for me?"

I hand her the huge gift bag. "Yeah."

"It's not my birthday," she says, smiling. Her eyes sparkle with such life, her cheeks flushed with happiness. And all I want to do is rip that tiny cardigan and dress off her. I'm better at the physical intimacy stuff.

I shove my hands in my pockets. "Just a small gift to thank you for the family room setup." *Any excuse.*

"But you haven't seen it yet! Come on!" She grabs my hand and pulls me with her.

I get to the family room, and she sets the bag down in the corner and immediately starts pointing everything out. "Same beautiful leather sofa with the pullout bed and now—matching recliner chairs and an ottoman." She goes over to Ace lounging on the ottoman. "Ace, off! I want to show him inside it."

Ace raises a brow, not wanting to give up his new cushy perch.

She scoops him up, tucking him against her shoulder and making kissy noises at him. "Go ahead and open it. There's storage."

"For what?"

"For whatever you want. Remote control, candles, blanket, whatever."

I peer inside the empty ottoman storage and close it again. "That could be good for your blanket and pillow." She sleeps on the sofa, and I find myself thinking about her down here while I'm upstairs way too much.

"Mmm-hmm, for now. And check out the end tables. Aren't they amazing? Adam Robinson made them. He's the master carpenter from Summerdale who did work on the inn too. Remember those built-in bookcases in the den?"

"I remember. Very cool. I didn't know you commissioned something special." I don't usually like surprises, but the end tables are a work of art. Modern with tapered legs and expertly crafted. I'm impressed.

She turns on the lamps on top of the tables, and they give off a soft glow through white shades. "Aren't they so hygge?"

"Depends on what hygge is."

"It's a Danish term, meaning cozy comfort. That's the vibe I'm going for while still being"—she lowers her voice to a gruff growl—"manly enough for you."

She rushes to the fireplace mantel. "And here's you and Livvie."

I walk over to inspect a photo of me and Livvie in a simple silver frame. I touch it, remembering her so little and vulnerable. Her quivering lower lip. She'd always come to me. Mom wasn't much comfort.

"Do you like it?" Skylar asks.

I like you. Too much. "It's great, Sky. Thank you." Ace squirms toward me from her arms, so I take him and give him a pet before setting him down. He doesn't like to be held all that much. He prefers to lie on my chest when I'm lying down on the sofa.

She beams her sunny smile at me, and my heart flips over. She does so much great stuff for me. I'm not even paying her. I should be the one doing stuff for her.

I gesture to the blank walls. "The only thing is, the walls are kinda empty."

She frowns. "You said you didn't want anything on the walls."

I walk over to the gift bag and hand it to her. "I changed my mind."

She opens the gift bag, her eyes widening. "Did you buy out the whole art store?"

"I didn't know exactly what you'd need, so I just got one of every kind of paint and a bunch of brushes. The saleslady said you'd probably want the palette sponges. There's a sketchpad, too, in case you start your paintings from sketches. I wasn't sure how you worked."

She beams another radiantly happy smile at me. "Thank you so much. It was so thoughtful of you."

I gesture vaguely. "I was hoping you could use the wall in here as your canvas."

"Are you serious? You want me to paint a mural here where you spend so much time?"

"Yes."

"I'd love to!" She hugs me, and I wrap my arms around her, a rare contentment settling into my bones.

She pulls away and gives me a mischievous smile. "I'm thinking whales."

"Whales, huh?"

"With a few dolphins and mermaids thrown in. Your guests will love it. I mean Livvie, since you don't have guests."

She's joking, but I'm serious about her expressing herself again through art. "Whatever you decide is fine by me."

"Wow. That's like letting someone else pick a tattoo for you. You'll have to look at it every day. Well, until you sell your house."

"Then you can paint a mural in my new house."

Her hand flies to her mouth, her eyes shining with unshed tears. I can't look away, even though my heart's in my throat.

Anything to keep you around. She'll only be here four weeks more at the most. I know exactly when she comes into the renovation schedule at Spencer and Paige's house since I made it. Then she'll move back to Summerdale and who knows where after that. "Anything you want. Really."

She turns to stare at the wall, her hand on her heart, before turning back to me. "This is the perfect gift."

My chest puffs with pride, that warm light feeling spreading through me again. I've never felt like this before, almost like a floating out-of-body experience as I watch her stare at the wall, her hand on her chin in deep thought. And it's enough.

Just being near her is enough. I never thought I could share my space with someone, let alone let them change things around and add their personal touch. But it makes her happy, and that's important. I almost wish I could go back and grant her every other decorating wish she had on our previous jobs. How crazy is that?

12

Skylar

Gage gave me free rein for the family room mural, so I painted my favorite spot in the world—Lake Summerdale. His gesture means so much to me, both because he believes in my abilities and because he trusts me. I know he plans to sell this place, so it's not like I'm making his home my home, but he did invite me to paint a mural at his new house too, which means something, right? I hug myself, a warm melty feeling flowing through me just thinking about Gage and the potential for more. The future is looking bright.

Almost as bright as this mural, a summer scene with gently rippling water surrounded by leafy green trees. On the water, there's kids splashing in the shallows, ducks and swans, and a few sailboats. On shore, there's families enjoying picnics, and off in a low corner in some tall grass, I added a tiny fairy. Only a little kid—maybe Gage's future niece or nephew—would notice the fairy hiding there. From an adult's height, it might appear to be a butterfly. Anyway, it's what I always wished to find when I was a kid. It's been five days from sketch to finished mural. I wanted it to be perfect, and I just finished it today.

The door opens from the garage. He's home! Ace leaves his favorite spot on the ottoman and trots over to the door. I bought champagne and chocolate-covered strawberries to celebrate the occasion. I'm a little nervous. If Gage likes the mural, we'll enjoy my celebration snack together, and if he doesn't, this will be my soothing snack alone in my room. Neurotic artist alert! It's been so long since I've painted anything this big. Either way, I'm just so happy to be painting again. I can't believe I neglected my arty side for so long.

I hurry into the kitchen to meet him.

His brown eyes are warm on mine. "Sky," he says in a husky voice full of warmth and sincerity. He greets me like this every time he comes home, like he's happy I'm here.

I smile and grab both of his hands, unable to contain my excitement. "It's done!"

"What's done? Another room or—"

"The mural! Come see. No, wait!" I go behind him and cover his eyes. "I need to make a grand reveal."

We make our awkward way through the empty dining area.

"You've been so secretive."

"Well, an artist needs space, especially the first time they tackle a mural in years." He's been hanging in his bedroom at night so he won't accidentally see it. I've been blocking his view whenever he goes into the kitchen. "And if you don't like any part of it, I can fix it. It's not hard to paint over something. And I'll take pictures of it too, so no worries if your new homeowners want to paint the whole wall white again. I won't be offended. I'm just happy to do it at all."

We head over to the family room separated only by a short wooden rail from the dining area. Ace tries to kill us on the way, looping around our legs.

I stop right in front of the mural and take my hands off his eyes. "Ta-dah!"

He's quiet.

My stomach drops. Does he hate it? I can't tell from his expression. He has resting stone face. "It's Lake Summerdale."

He moves closer to it, taking it in and moving from one

end to the other, and then backs up to take it in as a whole. "Is this the view you had growing up?"

"Yes. I find it so peaceful, and I hoped you would too."

He rubs his scruffy jaw. "You know what's missing?"

I scan the mural. It seems complete to me. "What?"

"Your signature. Sky, this is a piece of art. I want everyone to know the artist who painted it."

Tears spring to my eyes, my throat tight with emotion. "I can do that."

I go to my paints and dip my brush in black. Then I sign it on the lower right corner on the opposite side of my hidden fairy.

Gage pulls his phone out and takes a bunch of pictures of the mural, and then he directs me into the shot too. I beam at the camera. *He likes it!*

He checks the pictures on his phone and raises his head, his eyes intent on mine. "Do you mind if I share this with my clients? I think a lot of people would like an original mural in their homes or businesses."

I smile, tears stinging my eyes. Happy tears. "Of course! Share away."

He starts tapping on his phone.

I practically float over to the kitchen and go to the refrigerator for my celebration stuff. I take out the box of chocolate-covered strawberries I picked up at a local chocolatier and take out the champagne. First things first. I unwrap the foil from the top of the bottle and then press on the cork, twisting the bottle.

Pop!

Ace barks like a maniac.

Gage turns at the sound. "Sounds like we're celebrating."

"Yes, c'mere." I pour champagne into whiskey glasses. Gage doesn't have wine or champagne glasses. I make a mental note to order some. You can't entertain properly without them.

He joins me on the other side of the island and takes his glass. "A toast to you, the talented artist."

I beam, nearly vibrating in excitement. "Thank you, and a

toast to you for reminding me what I love to do and giving me a chance." We clink glasses and drink. Then I open the box of chocolate-covered strawberries and offer it to him.

"This looks like a real dessert," he says.

"But still with a healthy component—fruit."

I take a seat at the island and finish my strawberry in two bites.

He sits next to me. "You make every day feel like a special occasion."

"I do?"

"Yeah. Like there's always something you find to get excited over, or you make something happen like when you made banana bread or when you got flowers at the supermarket."

"That feels like a special occasion to you?"

He nods and bites into his strawberry treat.

"That's just regular life. A special occasion is more like champagne and decadent chocolate or presents!"

He swivels on his chair, shifting to face me. "I'm kinda getting used to having you around."

"So you don't hate it?" That's how he says he likes something—I don't hate it. I'm figuring out his alpha-male dialect.

"I don't hate it," he confirms.

"That's good because I'm here for three more weeks."

He sips champagne. "Then you'll go back to your brother's place while you work on Spencer and Paige's house, right?"

"That's the plan." I sip champagne, delighting in the fizzy bubbles and the way it sparkles in the light. What a fantastic day.

"And then what?"

"I'm hoping to have enough in the bank to get another apartment. I was renting a condo in Greenwich before, where I worked, but the owner decided to sell, and since I couldn't afford to buy it, I had to move out. This coincided with my unfortunate lack of work."

"It's hard to believe someone as talented as you doesn't have clients lining up down the street."

My cheeks heat. Both at the compliment and because I'm embarrassed about the reason for my current lack of clients. I finish my champagne and pour myself another.

He finishes his off, and I pour him one too.

He clinks his glass against mine, his gaze heated. Flutters in my stomach tell me something has shifted here. Gage has been careful around me ever since I told him we should back it up for both of our sakes. Not cross lines that can't be uncrossed. I've felt warmth from him, but not heat. Still, we've become closer. Every night at dinner he asks me to share something about myself, and then he shares. Just small things like my favorite music, favorite memory, what I'd do with a million dollars. I guessed his million-dollar wish too. I said he'd buy a house for Livvie and set her up with a trust fund. She's his top priority in life. Well, besides Ace.

I feel close to him, I think I can trust him, and the attraction is pulling me to him like a magnet. Forces beyond my control. "We've gotten to know each other better. A lot better."

"Yup. I know your favorite music is old-school Simon and Garfunkel, which shouldn't have been a surprise considering I had you pegged as a bohemian hippie from the start. Too bad you missed the '60s. You would've been in your element. And you'd give your million dollars to international disaster relief."

"Yes, and I'd save some for the animal shelter in Summerdale. Dr. Russo is doing great work over there."

He sips champagne and eyes me over the rim of the glass. "You smell like warm spice."

"Thank you. You smell woodsy and masculine, something uniquely you." I lean toward his neck and breathe in.

His hand cups the back of my neck, and he touches his forehead to mine. "Sky."

"Yes?"

"I respect the hell out of you."

I pull away, already knowing where this is going. He's about to tell me we should stay friends. I push down the hurt.

Gage thinks things through, much more than I do, and he's concluded we're better off just as we are. Maybe he's right.

Or not. My throat tightens. I don't even know anymore.

I walk to the other side of the island and help myself to another chocolate-covered strawberry, letting the deliciousness of sweet strawberry and rich chocolate soothe me.

After a long moment, he says, "It's not that you're not incredibly sexy—"

"We should get some dinner," I say brightly.

"I'll take you out. Somewhere nice. Let me just shower and change real quick."

I force a smile. "Sure, take your time." Obviously we're not in the same place. I have feelings, and he doesn't return them. These things can't be wished into existence.

He hesitates and closes the distance between us, his arm snaking around my waist and pulling me close. "Normally I'd take your cheerfulness as status quo, but I get the feeling you're not happy with me at the moment."

I lean back, trying to put some space between us, but he's got me in a firm grip. I give up and make a futile attempt to ignore the delicious feeling of being pressed against his hard warm chest. "Why would you say that? I'm fine."

"You're not fine."

I push at his chest. "You're giving me mixed signals. You hold me close, but you just want to be friends or whatever. Just let me go."

"I don't want to be friends. A woman friend is the last thing I need." He sighs so big it parts my hair. "I can't handle hurting you. You're all open loving sunshine, and I'm…not."

I swallow hard. "It's true we're opposites, but I thought we were starting to understand each other."

"There's a reason none of my relationships work out."

"I told you Kate wasn't your fault."

He looks to the ceiling and then levels me with a hard look. "No promises. Whatever your expectations are, lower them."

I don't like the sound of that at all. I lift my chin. "You're right. This would never work. Excuse me. I've got work to do upstairs."

"What about dinner?"

I grab the box of strawberries and the bottle of champagne. "All set."

≈

Gage

I did the right thing keeping my distance from Skylar. I know I did. So why do I still feel like shit two days later? I disappointed her, but wouldn't it be worse to hurt her down the line? My one and only serious relationship crashed and burned, and even if it wasn't my fault Kate had to go to therapy, it still ended terribly. Kate and I lashed out at each other during the month I still had to work on her house.

Before Kate, nothing else went beyond a third date. It must be me who's the problem. Now it's Friday night, and Skylar and I are supposed to go on a double date with Livvie and Charles. I'm not sure if Skylar will even want to go. She's been keeping to herself, not even joining me for dinner.

God, I miss her.

I miss her warmth, her beaming smiles, her energy and enthusiasm. I miss talking to her, sharing meals, even watching TV together. She got me hooked on this reality show where they hunt for a house in an exotic location. It's cool to see the different house styles in other parts of the world. Even Ace misses her, going upstairs and whining outside her door.

I knock on the door of her home office upstairs. She opens it a moment later, wearing a flowing white peasant blouse and a black pencil skirt with heels. Her hair is down in tousled waves. She takes my breath away.

"I didn't forget about our double date," she says, brushing past me. "Let's go."

I'm so relieved she's not bailing on me with Livvie, I have the urge to grab her in a hug. Instead I follow her downstairs, restraining myself with iron willpower. Touching her is like touching fire—dangerous and someone's going to get burned.

I'm starting to think that someone is me. I'm the one all twisted up inside.

"Thank you," I say once we're in my truck.

"I'm just here to balance things out. You're the one who needs to make up with Livvie and Charles."

I know that, but I don't know exactly how to do that. I head over to the Italian restaurant in town, where Livvie and Charles are meeting us. Skylar's so uncharacteristically quiet I actually attempt small talk.

"How was your day?" I ask.

"Good. I already texted you the update on your formal living room and office. The desk and assorted accent tables are in place. Still have to wait another couple of weeks for the sofa and love seat. No color on the walls, as you requested. I added area rugs to the order, but I'll remove them if you don't like them."

"I'm sure they'll be great."

"Mmm-hmm." She looks out the window.

"Are you mad at me?"

"Why would I be mad at you?"

That sounds like a trap. Like she wants me to give her a reason to be mad at me. "I don't know."

She's quiet again.

She's mad all right. But wouldn't she be more mad if things didn't work out, which they probably wouldn't since they never do. Then what? We're at each other's throats for the rest of this job and the next on Spencer and Paige's house. I don't want a repeat of the Kate disaster.

I pull into the restaurant parking lot and spot Livvie and Charles waiting out front. It's a cold night. Livvie should be inside keeping warm.

Skylar gets out of the truck before I have a chance to open her door for her. I walk alongside her to the front entrance, and she speeds up.

"Hi, Livvie! Hi, Charles!" she exclaims more cheerfully than she spoke to me today. "Great to see you." She hugs Livvie and then gives Charles a hug too.

A sudden heaviness in my body makes me want to go

back to my comfortable sofa with Ace, but I'm here now, things are complicated, and I have to straighten it all out. I'm so frigging tired of having to fix problems all the time.

"Hi, Gage," Livvie says in a subdued tone.

"You should be inside. It's cold out."

"I'm wearing a coat in case you didn't notice," she says tightly.

I turn to Charles, trying to muster up a greeting, but every time I look at his bearded face, I think, *There's the guy trying to ruin my sister's future.*

"Hi," he says.

"Let's go in." I open the door to the restaurant and wait for them all to file in. Skylar doesn't even glance at me.

This is Livvie's favorite restaurant, which is why I picked it. I give my name to the host for our reservation.

We're shown to a table for four in the private back dining area. There's only one other group here, so it's pretty quiet. Charles takes off Livvie's coat for her and sets it on the back of her chair; then he helps her into her chair. She smiles up at him. I turn to Skylar, but she's already seated, shrugging out of her coat.

I take a seat. It's a square table with Skylar by my side and the happy couple on the other side.

The waiter stops by to see if we want drinks and to tell us about the specials. Livvie orders a glass of merlot. Charles sticks to water since he's driving, which I appreciate. I'm tempted to tell him that, but I'm not sure if it's the right thing to say. It might come off sounding too dad-like.

"I'll have a pineapple martini," Skylar says.

"Just water for me," I say.

As soon as the waiter leaves, Skylar says to Livvie, "I could use a drink. It's been that kind of day."

I turn to her. "What happened?" She didn't say a word about any issues on the drive here, and I asked her how her day was too.

She waves that away. "Have you two set a date?"

I cut that off before Livvie can get too carried away.

"How're your studies? You have midterms coming up soon, right?"

Livvie presses her lips together. "You know, pretending I'm not engaged doesn't make it true."

I take a deep breath. "I'm not pretending. I just want to know how school's going."

"Fine."

"Livvie's the smartest one in our class," Charles puts in.

I give him a sour look. *No one asked you, Charles*. Obviously I know my sister's smart. She earned a merit scholarship.

Skylar sits back with a sigh and studies the menu.

An awkward silence follows.

Livvie and Charles exchange a look before turning to their menus. Skylar looks checked out. *Aren't I going to get any help here?* This was Skylar's idea, and now she's abandoning me. Does she actually think I know how to keep my sister from screwing up her life without pissing her off?

Long moments tick by, and it's a relief when the waiter arrives with our drinks. We all take a long drink right away.

"Need a moment?" the waiter asks.

"We're ready." I just want to get through this tense meal as quickly as possible.

The waiter turns to Livvie first. She smiles sweetly. "I'll have the eggplant parmigiana."

"What happened to chicken marsala?" I ask. "That's your favorite."

"Charles and I are vegetarian now."

"Whose idea was that?" *Already he's trying to change her!*

Charles responds in an irritatingly calm voice, "We've been studying nutrition and thought it would be healthier." He turns to the waiter. "I'll have the same."

"I'll just have a salad," Skylar says.

My head whips toward hers. "What do you mean just a salad?" I've seen her eat a hearty portion every night at dinner.

"I'm not very hungry," she says.

"And you, sir?" the waiter asks.

I slowly turn to him, convinced Skylar's mad at me.

Clearly she's going to be no help tonight. "I'll have the rib eye, medium."

The waiter quickly leaves.

I stare at Charles. Maybe we could come up with some kind of contract spelling out the terms for being with my sister. If he agrees to wait five years to marry Livvie, so she can graduate and have a solid foundation independent of him, I'll give him my stamp of approval. That seems like a win-win.

But would it make Livvie mad if I went straight to Charles man-to-man? Maybe a separate contract with Livvie spelling out similar, and I'll throw in money for the wedding? That way everyone is treated equally with the same goal in mind. Damn, I wish Skylar had still been having dinner with me these past couple of nights. This is exactly the kind of thing she could've helped with.

Before I can decide which one of them to approach about the contract first, Livvie asks Skylar about her work on my house, and Skylar finally shows signs of life, showing her pictures of what she's done so far.

"I love this mural!" Livvie exclaims. "Did you do this?"

"Yes," Skylar says modestly. "It's the view of the lake I grew up on."

Livvie takes the phone to look closer, enlarging the picture. She laughs. "You have a little orange fairy hiding in the grass. Did you notice this, Gage?"

"Fairy?" I mutter. "No."

Skylar smiles at her. "I was always hunting for fairies as a kid. I put it low enough that only a little kid would notice."

Livvie gives Skylar a curious look and then turns to me. I pull my collar away from my heated neck. Whose kid are we talking about here? It's not like that with me and Skylar. Is that what she wants?

There's a fairy on my wall?

"I love it," Livvie says. "You were so lucky to grow up with this view."

"Our house was right off the shore. I always did feel lucky."

This is a touchy subject for Skylar since she lost her home to a bulldozer. I try to shift the topic. "She's a very talented artist."

Skylar meets my eyes for an intense heated moment. "Thank you."

I'm so relieved to feel that connection with her again, I want to give her more compliments, but now is not the time.

The women turn to each other, talking like old friends. I've got nothing to say to Charles.

By the time dinner arrives, things go downhill fast. Both Livvie and Charles are eying me with my giant steak. Skylar finished her salad in a few bites and is gazing out the window in the back of the room. I don't know what she's looking at. It's dark outside.

"So, Skylar, you've been living with Gage for two and a half weeks. How do you like it?"

"The sofa is very comfortable," Skylar says flatly.

Livvie and Charles exchange another look. Did they think Skylar and I were a couple now? Well, I guess a double date would suggest that. But this was all Skylar's idea to smooth things over with Livvie. And she's not helping me at all!

"Getting along?" Livvie asks.

"Sure," Skylar says.

Livvie shoots me a dark look.

What?

Her eyes flash, but she doesn't say anything.

I sit straighter and get to the point of tonight's meal. "Look, I've thought about it, and I'm okay with you being engaged as long as you promise not to get married until after you graduate and have a job."

"Thanks, *Dad*," Livvie replies sarcastically.

"Would you like to stop by the prison to ask for his permission?" I shoot back. The moment the words are out of my mouth, I regret them. "Sorry."

"I don't need anyone's permission! In case you haven't noticed, I'm a fully grown adult." She tosses her napkin on the table and stands. "We're leaving."

I jump up. "Livvie, wait."

She shakes her head and walks out with Charles. I turn to Skylar, who gives me a blank look. No help there.

I jog after Livvie. "Just listen for a minute. Don't go like this."

Charles checks in with her.

"It's okay," Livvie tells him. "I'll meet you at the car."

We go outside to the sidewalk. She shivers in the cold and wraps her coat more tightly around her. "Well?"

I struggle to find the words. "I don't want to fight."

"Me either."

"I want you to be happy, but I also want you to have a stable future."

"What do you think marriage is?"

"You know what I mean. I want you to graduate and be financially independent so you'll never end up like Mom." My voice chokes. The one thing I've been trying to prevent is happening before my eyes.

"Oh, Gage. I'm nothing like her, and I promise you my eyes are wide open. Charles is a great guy, he really is, and if you gave him a chance, you'd see that future with him is the best thing that's ever happened to me. He's a rock-solid, stable guy. There's nothing to worry about here."

I stare at her, still not convinced. "I'm glad you're happy."

She smiles. "I'm so happy."

"But you can't get married until you graduate." I'm giving a lot here, dropping the *having a job* clause in hopes of salvaging what I can.

She rolls her eyes. "We planned to wait until after graduation to get married, I'm not sure when, but it would be nice if we both had steady jobs first. And that's not because of you. It's just the sensible thing to do."

"Oh."

"Just 'oh'?"

My throat tightens. "You know I'm not good with words." I pull her close and give her a tight hug, kissing the top of her head. "I'm glad you're so sensible."

She looks up at me, smiling. "I really like Skylar. You should give *her* a few more words. I don't think it would take much for her to give you a second chance. You obviously did something to piss her off."

I drop my arms from her and rub the back of my neck, not too surprised Livvie picked up on the fact that I screwed up with Skylar. "Yeah, well, it's complicated."

"Doesn't need to be. You two had a moment there when you bragged about her being an artist. I think friendship and mutual admiration could be a good start to something real."

"Maybe I'm not cut out for relationships."

"Of course you are! God, Kate really did a number on you. I want to throw her off a cliff for that."

"Wow, Liv, I thought you were all about caring and nurturing other people."

"Which I learned from you! You're the one who was there for me day in and day out, loving and supporting me."

A sliver of hope shines through. Maybe I'm not death to relationships. My hope dims just as quickly. "That's different. We're blood."

"Yes, it is different, but it's still love."

I shake my head. "I'm not in love." *Am I?* Is that why I miss Skylar so much, even when she's right upstairs? The reason every time I come home from work and see her there, all the tension leaves my body, replaced with a light, weightless feeling. I've never felt like this before. Being with Kate was a roller coaster of ups and downs. But Skylar is... sunshine and rainbows. I actually like sunshine and rainbows now. More than like. I *need* them in my life.

"I'm going to go." Livvie gives my shoulder a shove. "Don't be an idiot."

And then she leaves. I watch as Charles hurries to meet her halfway, putting his arm around her and guiding her to his car, an old Honda Civic. Seems his intentions are good. And Livvie's happy.

I return to our table and flag down the waiter to pay the bill, giving him my credit card. As soon as he leaves, I turn to Skylar, who's scrolling on her phone. "Livvie says I'm an idiot."

She doesn't bother to look up from her screen. "Oh, yeah?"

"Yeah."

"Hmm…"

"Not going to disagree?"

"I don't want to be rude." Finally, she looks at me, her expression bland. "You're my client, and soon we'll be coworkers again. Let's keep things civil."

"So you do think I'm an idiot."

She goes back to her phone.

I exhale sharply. The waiter returns with my credit card; I take care of the bill and turn to Skylar. "Ready?"

She stands and puts her jacket on. "Yes. Thanks for dinner."

"You're welcome."

We walk out together. She's quiet, which makes me want to fill the silence.

"You didn't seem like you enjoyed dinner much," I say.

"I was just here to help your sister feel comfortable, so it would be balanced. The rest was on you."

We get to the truck, and I open the door for her, wait for her to get in, and shut it behind her, my mind whirling with thoughts of my talk with Livvie. I was able to work through a sensible plan with Livvie. Now to do the same with Skylar.

Once I'm back on the road, I say, "I've missed seeing you at dinner."

"You saw me tonight."

"Yeah." I search my brain for how to say I like sunshine and rainbows without actually saying sunshine and rainbows. Something that will show her I have feelings for her. God, I *have* been an idiot. She won't be at my place forever. I can't let the closeness we had get away from me. It's so rare. A gift.

I clear my throat. "You know, I've been thinking and, uh, no rush to finish the job at my place." Dammit. That's not what I meant to say.

"Everything's on track. I'm actually ahead of schedule

since your furniture arrived so quickly. By the way, I won't be around for a few days."

I sit straighter. *Is it because of me?* "Why?"

"I'm going to stay at my brother's place while I paint a mural for the Inn at Lovers' Lane."

I look over at her. "Really? That's great."

She gives me a small smile. "I know you told Spencer to hire me. You guys are friends."

"I swear I didn't. I just sent him and Paige a picture of your work." *And told them how amazing you are.*

"I appreciate your little promo of my work. They want me to paint a mural in the dining area of the inn. They have a historic photo of the original Dutch farmhouse surrounded by farmland that they want me to use as inspiration. That way it'll give the guests a sense of the inn's history."

A rush of affection takes me by surprise, like I want to hold her close, just hold her. "I'm so proud of you."

"Thanks. I'm proud of me too."

"So I guess I'll see you in a few days."

"Mmm-hmm."

"Once you get back, you could, uh, stay longer at my place if you wanted."

She studies me for a long moment. "That's okay. We'll just stick to our original agreement. Six weeks."

My gut does a slow churn. We only have three weeks left. It's not enough. Just the thought of my house without Skylar makes me feel lonely. I never felt lonely in all the years I've lived alone before.

But how do I get her to stay?

13

Skylar

I'm having a blast painting the bucolic scene of the inn back when it was a farm. It's cool to imagine my hometown back in the 1700s. It's still beautiful now too. It must've been kinda lonely back then when there were only a few farms with long distances between them. On horseback, it would've taken a while just to go into town for supplies. I'm too used to an instant-gratification lifestyle, but there's something so peaceful about stepping into this scene.

So far I have rolling hills, the treeline, and the broad strokes of the farmhouse. This mural, though smaller than the one at Gage's house, is taking a little longer because I did some research on Summerdale in the olden days, going through the archives at Town Hall and what Audrey dug up for me at the library.

I rinse my brushes and stretch. Time for a break. It's late Wednesday afternoon, so I've got time to peek next door at the renovations on Spencer and Paige's house. Who knows, maybe I'll be inspired to tweak the design a bit for their house. Wouldn't that be just what Gage wants to hear? I smile to myself. He's still rigid, but I've seen glimpses of a tender caring side. He said he missed seeing me at dinner. I was hurt by his rejection initially, though as rejections go "I respect the hell out of you" is a good one. I've made peace with it. If it's meant to be, it will be.

Yeah, easy to be philosophical about it when I haven't seen him for a few days. I miss him.

A few minutes later, I knock on the front door of Paige and Spencer's house and then let myself in. I can hear the nail gun inside, which means it's hard to hear someone at the door. "Hellooo!" I call, announcing myself.

"Hey, Skylar," a guy from crew says. "Big man's upstairs."

"Oh, I'm not here to see Gage. I just wanted to check out the progress in here."

"Just adding the frames to the new windows." He gestures to where he was nailing the wooden sill to a window.

"Kitchen done?"

He gestures for me to check it out, so I do.

Nice. It had to be a gourmet kitchen to satisfy chef Spencer. It's still bare bones. No countertops. Just cabinets, a farmhouse sink, and a center prep island. The ceramic tile floor I ordered is in place. I'll be back to check on the new paint color, granite countertops, backsplash, and cabinet pulls.

I go to the living room. "Sounds like everyone else is upstairs."

"Yup. Working on the master suite."

I start up the stairs just as Gage appears at the top of them. "Hi!"

"Sky! What're you doing here?" He sounds happy to see me as he heads down the steps.

I turn and walk back to the main floor, stopping in the front hall. "I'm painting the mural next door and wanted to check out the progress over here."

"Everything's on schedule."

"I expected no less. I'll check in with the painter for the downstairs."

"Already covered. He'll be here tomorrow."

"Oh, good."

"I'm on break. Mind if I check out your mural?"

"It's not finished."

"That's even more interesting. Last time I only saw the finished project. This time I can see how it comes together."

"Well, okay, if you want."

He holds the front door open for me and joins me outside. "It's been quiet at my house without you. Ace is confused where all the fun went."

I laugh. "Ace misses me, huh?"

"Yeah, there's been a lot of pacing and looking out the front window for the past three nights. Ace too."

I laugh out loud. *He missed me.* "I'll be back in a couple more days if everything goes as expected here. It's not as big a mural as I did for you, but it took more research to be historically accurate."

"Guess I'm the lucky one with the biggest signed Skylar Bellamy original."

My cheeks flush. "Guess so."

"Mark my words, people will know your name."

I give him a little shove. "Stop."

He laughs. "Seriously."

We head for the street to avoid the muddy grassy area connecting the home and the inn's property. Now that it's March, the snow's melting.

"How's Livvie?" I ask.

"She started texting me again, so that's something."

"Just try not to be so you, and she'll come around."

"That sounds so reassuring."

I laugh. "It was meant to be."

"And how exactly can I not be so me?"

"Just chill a bit. Like me. Relaxed and easy. Go with the flow. Take life as it comes with open arms and a smile."

"So you want me to be Mr. Perky?"

"You'd have to marry me first!" I grin, but he doesn't smile back; instead he looks damn serious. "Kidding!"

He grunts.

No idea what that grunt meant. Is he into the idea of a committed, long-term relationship with me? Did our time apart change his perspective on things?

"Here we are!" I open the door to the inn with a flourish.

There's a couple on the sofa in the living room. Guess the guests came downstairs.

I walk in. "Hi, I'm Skylar. I'm the one working on the mural. Just brought my friend from next door to check it out."

"It's beautiful so far," the woman says.

Gage raises a hand in greeting and walks over to the mural.

The guy gestures to it. "We were looking at the photograph you're working from. You really made the old black-and-white picture come to life, like it would've been back in colonial times."

"Thanks so much! Like I said, it's not finished, but if you'll be around on Saturday, I should be done by then."

"We'll look forward to it," the woman says.

"Thanks!" I join Gage by the painting and show him the historic photograph. "I still need to add in the apple and pear trees over here. I'm going to paint a couple of dogs, cows, horses, sheep, a farmer with his plow, and I'm considering a horse and carriage out front like someone is just returning home. I like the idea of the inn being a place you come home to."

He searches my expression before saying, "This picture is in the dead of winter, yet you made it come to life in summer."

"Just takes a little imagination. Besides, I know what Summerdale looks like in all seasons, and I did my research for historical accuracy." I gesture to the sky in the painting. "This is my favorite kind of cloud, so I was generous with the white fluffiness against the sky."

He gestures toward the tree line in back. "It looks just like when the sun filters through the leaves."

"I told you I know this town. My brothers and I spent so much time outside at the lake, exploring, digging in the sand, splashing each other, and swimming. It's in my blood. One day I'd love to buy a house on the lake again. Though the way things are going, the smaller places are getting snatched up quick by people in the city looking for a summer home or to bulldoze and build something big."

"Like what happened to your family home."

I nod, my mood dimming as it always does when I think of the destruction of my beloved lake house. I know it was only from the '60s, but in a way it was historic. In the olden days, Summerdale was just farms and a stagecoach stop. It was those hippies like my grandfather who made it a town. They wanted to build utopia. Those lakeside cottages were the original founders' homes.

"Seems like there should be some historic preservation at play here," he says.

I'm surprised we're thinking along the same lines. "I don't think the homes are old enough."

"Someone should preserve at least one of the homes to mark the founding of the town. I'll look into it."

"But you don't even live here."

"Doesn't hurt to ask. I've got contacts with the town building department since I'm working on my third project in town."

"Thanks," I say softly, touched that he cares.

He inclines his head and turns back to the mural. "Keep going. You've got something special here, and don't forget to sign it. You can add it to your website in a special section for murals."

"Great idea. Okay, I'm going to get started again. I'll see you back at your place probably on Saturday."

He slowly backs away, watching me. "Take breaks. Don't wear yourself out."

"The more I paint, the more energy I get."

"Did you eat lunch?"

I laugh. "Yes, I ate lunch!" So sweet the way he looks after me. I'm so glad I got to see him today.

I turn to the mural and study it for a moment before rushing to my paints to add shadow to the side of the house.

～

Just as I'm finishing a simple stir-fry dinner back at the studio apartment behind my brother's house, my sister-in-law

Brooke stops by. She's a practical woman, an architect and part-time innkeeper, with straight dark brown hair and pretty green eyes.

She hugs me the moment she steps inside. "We missed you around here. Max says you've been staying with a friend in New Jersey while you work on a project there."

Yup, that's the updated story I gave my brother, and he never asked which friend. Unlike Gage with his sister, Max is content to take me at my word with no further follow-up. He's laid-back until you set off his big-brother radar. In any case, enough time has passed since Valentine's Day that I'm not so worried about Brett showing up here. Still, I'll be going back to Gage's place to finish my work there and to see if things have changed between us. Maybe we just needed a little time apart to realize how much we wanted to be together. I'm ready to take the leap of faith that things will work out.

"I'll be back here in a little over two weeks to finish up the work on Spencer and Paige's house," I say. "Then I'll be looking for my next client and a new apartment."

She squeezes my arm. "The mural you're working on is even better than I imagined. You should include murals in your interior design service."

"I plan to. It's the most fun I've had in a long time."

"Awesome. Maybe you've found your calling. If you want, I could let my brother, Wyatt, know about your work. He's well connected with a ton of wealthy people, including contacts in the city." New York City being "the city" around here.

"That would be great. As long as he's up to it with the baby." I heard Wyatt and Sydney are sleep deprived from their newborn daughter, Quinn. She's eight weeks old and a screamer.

"I'll check. In the meantime, I just stopped by because a bunch of us are heading to beginner karate class tonight to spy on Audrey and Drew. You should join us. It'll be fun."

"Does Audrey know everyone's going to spy on her?"

She grins. "Actually, she invited us to learn self-defense

because she's really into it for reasons she won't admit to." She coughs out, "Drew." He's the owner of the dojo.

"Seemed like he just wanted to be friends."

"You didn't hear this from me, but Audrey confessed to my sister, who shared with my other blabbermouth sister, that Audrey thinks there *might* be something there this time, so we're going to check out the dynamic and report back."

That's the small-town grapevine for you. I feel bad for Audrey. It must be horrible to have a lifelong crush who always puts you in the friend zone except for occasional bright moments of hope that string you along.

"Sure," I say. "It'll be fun."

"Great! You can ride over with me. It's at seven."

"I'll be ready."

"Oh, and before you leave again, I wanted to go over your business and marketing plan. Did you have a chance to read the articles I emailed you?" Max made her do that. I know because he keeps following up with me.

"No, but I already have a plan."

"Great! Can't wait to see it. I told Max you had this covered."

I repress a sigh. Big bro is still checking up on me, but how can I tell her no? That'll only send Max over here to find out why. That secret stays with me.

I've never been to a karate class before. It's an interesting setup. There's a large ring, almost like a boxing ring, with a bouncy floor and multiple freestanding punching bags along the front of it. The regular students are wearing a white karate uniform, most of them are white belts, including Audrey. The rest of us—the Audrey posse—are just wearing casual T-shirts and jogging pants or shorts.

Drew walks onto the mat with a confident swagger, his dark eyes sharp as he directs us to line up for warm-up exercises. He's in a white uniform that contrasts with his tanned skin and dark hair. His belt is black with multiple embroidered bars on it. I think that might indicate degrees of black belt.

The regulars from class bow to him and say, "Yes, Sensei!"

Wow, hardcore.

"Welcome to the newcomers," Drew says. "I hope you'll all get something out of it."

After some stretches, Drew demonstrates a few holds and how to get out of them. He uses another guy in class and then has us practice on each other. It's hard to do when we're all craning our necks to see how Drew acts around Audrey. She's one hundred percent enthusiasm and focus.

In fact, Audrey has become a badass. She gets out of a hold and takes down her female partner with a loud "kyah!" No sign of the buttoned-up librarian here today.

"Good," Drew tells her casually before moving to the next person. He's making the rounds, and Audrey is just another student to him.

I'm partnered up with Sloane, who's a petite brunette and unexpectedly strong. I land on the floor with a thud. *Ow.*

"Sorry!" she says, looking down at me. "I didn't mean to throw you so hard. I'm used to lifting heavy car parts."

"No problem. That's great that you're so strong."

She offers her hand and helps me up.

"Oh, you must be Mr. Murray's daughter. I just put that together. Weren't you a model when you were younger? I remember kids on the playground mentioning you went to the city for glamorous modeling gigs."

"Not that glamorous," she mutters.

"Talk on your own time," Drew barks. "Focus, ladies!"

Sloane widens her eyes at me comically, and I stifle a laugh.

Jenna and Kayla are paired up, which is funny because Jenna's a tall thin blonde and Kayla is a petite brunette. We watch and...yes, Kayla does it. Jenna takes a fall to the mat in what looks like a graceful dance move. Kayla beams and offers her hand to help her up.

Drew's in the front row, correcting someone's takedown

maneuver, so I lean over and whisper to Kayla, "That looked like a choreographed fall."

"It was," Kayla whispers back. "Jenna just found out she's pregnant, and we didn't want to shake the baby."

Jenna elbows her. "I should've known you couldn't keep it a secret."

Kayla slaps a hand over her mouth. "I didn't know it was a secret."

"My hubby wants to wait to tell people until I'm farther along," Jenna says. "Not even his family knows."

Paige walks over. "We should be partners then, since we're both preggos." She and Jenna start whispering about pregnancy.

Drew stalks toward the group of us. "I'd appreciate your focus on class, ladies."

Audrey looks back at us with a glare. *What? We came here for her benefit.* She invited us out of enthusiasm for self-defense, but we're going to help her figure out the more crucial problem of Drew. Why does he want to keep her in the friend zone when she's such a catch? Isn't it every guy's fantasy to watch a reserved librarian let down their hair? She's pretty, smart, and kind. And it's so obvious she's into him, even after all these years. Hopelessly devoted is not a good look for anyone.

"Yes, sir," Jenna says with a note of irony. They grew up together.

"Sensei will suffice," Drew says sharply. He claps and strides to the front. "Okay, now we're going to cover some basic kicks."

The rest of class goes smoothly. We all like doing kicks, and it's even more fun when Drew and another helper guy from class roll the punching bags out for us to practice on. I'm channeling my inner Wonder Woman strength and badassery. *Hi-yah!* I should've worn my Wonder Woman panties for this!

We finish class with a cooldown and a thank-you to our teacher. Drew follows us off the mat to invite us to return next week.

"You should," Audrey says to us. "It's a great class."

Drew gestures to Audrey. "If someone her size can handle this, any of you ladies can."

Audrey frowns.

I can't help but chime in, "How can I get as badass as Audrey?"

"Practice." Drew turns to Audrey. "Good work, Aud, keep it up. You'll be a yellow belt in no time."

Audrey looks up at him under her lashes. "I might even stick around long enough to be a black belt."

"Great." He addresses all of us. "I encourage all of my students to stick with it."

Audrey's voice drops to a husky whisper. "It could take years."

Drew nods once. "Probably will."

Clueless.

"Okay, then," Audrey says, turning on her heel and walking over to the waiting area to get her shoes and socks from a cubby shelf. We all follow her, putting our stuff back on too. She's quietly pissed, and I don't blame her. There was definitely nothing less than professionalism from Drew.

We all meet up outside.

"I was wrong," Audrey says flatly. "There's nothing going on."

"It seemed like he was happy with your progress," Kayla says diplomatically.

Dead silence. There's just nothing positive to add.

"I'm not going back to class until after the baby's born," Paige says.

"Me neither," Jenna says. "I was just here to see what the deal was with Drew. So, let's see, the man blocks Levi from asking you out, invites you here, and sells you on a bunch of classes while keeping you permanently in the friend zone. That's some marketing plan."

Audrey sighs. "That about sums it up. He's nothing but professional. I don't know why I thought otherwise."

"So disappointing," I say. "Seems like it's time to move on. Levi really is a nice guy."

Audrey smooths her dark hair back, blinking rapidly. "Levi is awesome, but I just don't feel that way about him."

Jenna squeezes her shoulder.

"I don't know why I'm disappointed," Audrey says. "I should've known Drew will always see me as his little sister's friend he has to look out for. That's what karate class means to him. He sees me as a little thing he needs to protect in some way."

I think of Gage and his protective love for his little sister. "Sometimes an older brother looks out for you because that's how he shows love. Like my two older brothers. Not in an oppressive way, just to make sure you're okay because they care. I think Drew sincerely cares about you."

Brooke and Paige exchange a look. "There's some truth to that," Paige says. "Wyatt still looks out for us."

"Overprotective older brother alert," Brooke says.

"Wyatt loves us with all of his heart," Kayla says, a hand to her heart.

Audrey gives them a small smile. "I'm an only child, so I guess I don't know that feeling. Drew is the oldest in his family, so maybe he does protect those he loves, but don't you see how that keeps me in the—" she finger quotes "—little-sister box? Kind of like an honorary little sister."

"There's definitely mixed signals here," Paige says. "I've seen him give you a smoldering look now and then at the bar. I don't think he thinks of you strictly in the sister box."

"Great!" Audrey says sarcastically. "After he has a few beers and is feeling lonely, then I step out of the little-sister box. Just what every woman wants. Beer-goggled love."

"Aww!" Kayla throws an arm around Audrey and gives her a sideways hug, and then her friends rush her for a group hug. I join in.

Audrey smiles. "Thanks, ladies. Anyone want to go back to my place for wine and chocolate? We've got to ruin this workout, right?"

"It's that kind of night," Jenna says. "I'm in, but I'll stick to sparkling water."

We all say a quick bye and head back to our cars to drive over to Audrey's place. I get into Brooke's car, thinking of that whole overprotective thing and the confusing mixed signals of guys who give you heated looks and then go out of their way to keep you safe, even from them. I know a little something about that.

But that's going to change soon. I'll make sure of it.

14

Gage

Skylar should be here any minute. It's Saturday night, and she's finally coming home from her work on the inn's mural. I bought candles and silver candlesticks for the center of the island. Her favorite Thai takeout waits on the side. I even set out plates and silverware ahead of time, side by side.

Embarrassingly enough, I'd gotten so used to coming home to her, I actually called out her name the first time I came home and she wasn't here. We talked on the phone every night, but it wasn't enough. I barely slept when she was away, remembering how it is when she's here—like a real home. Ace missed her too, crying outside Skylar's room every night. Now's the time to make my move, and I just hope I don't screw this up. Nerves run through me, and I pace the front hall.

Ace watches me curiously from the end of the hall closest to the kitchen, his pointy ears up and his head cocked sideways.

"She'll be here soon," I tell him.

It took Skylar longer to finish the mural today than she originally thought because she kept finding inspiring new details to add. I'm glad she's happily lost in her work, but come on already. I finally figured out I have feelings, deep feelings, and I have to say something about them. This time I'm going to share from the heart. I'm not going to assume she knows how I feel. That's the mistake I made with Kate.

I halt and exhale sharply. If things go sideways with Skylar, I'll just back off. No fault, no blame. I'll stay out of her way at Spencer and Paige's house during the renovation. I'll come in extra early in the morning when she's not there just to make things easier for her.

And if things don't go sideways, maybe, just maybe, she'll stay with me.

I run my clammy hands on my jeans, jittery and tense like I'm on a first date back in high school. But the stakes are so much higher, I'm talking the deep end—

I'm going to invite her to move in with me.

Adrenaline jolts me at the thought, and I do a quick walk around the downstairs, making sure everything looks good for her arrival. Why am I so nervous? It's not like anything's changed. That she knows of, anyway, but on the inside, I'm having all sorts of feelings I didn't know I was capable of. I think I'm in love with her. Why else am I a bundle of nerves, my thoughts jumping all over the place?

Ace suddenly bolts toward the front door, barking. It's her! I flush hot and smooth my short hair back. Then I take off my flannel shirt so I'm just in a T-shirt. Maybe I should've dressed up.

She unlocks the door with the key I gave her and appears a moment later, holding out her palm for Ace to sniff. "It's just me, boy. Miss me?"

Her long hair is down, falling in a silky cascade. Her coat is open, revealing an oversized white blouse and black leggings. Her feet are in sexy leopard-print ankle boots.

I cross to her, taking her suitcase and bag. "Ace missed you like crazy." *Just like me.* "He kept running to the door with every little sound, hoping it was you." I leave out how he cried every night. It's uncomfortably close to my own aching to see her again.

"Aww!" She crouches down and gives him some love, petting his head and behind his ears.

"I missed you too," I admit, wanting some of that affection for myself.

She looks up at me, smiling. "Yeah?"

"Yeah." Heat creeps up my neck. She didn't say she missed me back. "I'll put these in your office upstairs. The daybed arrived, and I set it up for you."

"So I finally graduate from the sofa."

I head upstairs so I don't blurt what I really want to say—you can stay with me in my bed.

I push open the bedroom where she's staying and set her stuff in there. It looks so lived in. Not messy so much as pure Skylar. It smells like lavender from the aromatherapy diffuser she loves to use. Various color samples are taped to the wall, and fabric samples are draped over a white project board. I put Livvie's pink and white polka-dot comforter on the bed. Skylar's been sleeping with a smaller throw blanket downstairs. I bet she'd choose a comforter with leopard print or rainbow tie-dye.

"Cute!" she says from behind me.

I whirl, surprised I didn't hear her approach.

"Darn, I should've brought my bedding with me. I left it at Max's cottage. Let me guess, this is Livvie's stuff."

"Yeah, it's all I had, but I can get you whatever you want. Or you can pick a different room." *Like mine. Am I really going to do this? Make the leap? I've never leaped without looking for a very long time.*

But I'm running out of time. Less than two weeks.

"This room's fine," she says. "My comforter is a soothing pale blue. I like cool colors in the bedroom."

There goes my leopard idea. Here I thought I knew her so well, but there's so much more to get to know. That just adds another reason to have her move in. It could take a long time to truly understand everything about her.

"Me too, I think. Is white a cool color?" Should I mention extending her stay with me, or just staying permanently? Maybe I should start with moving forward with us. I'm not sure the timing is right for any of that stuff. My emotions are clouding my normal orderly thinking process. So damn

inconvenient all these emotions. I need clarity again. I need to
know we're on the same page.

"Works for me," she says.

"I got pad Thai for dinner. You hungry?"

"Starving!"

She heads downstairs, and I follow. Ace is waiting for us
at the bottom of the stairs and rolls over at Skylar's feet,
begging for a tummy rub. She sits on the last step and obliges
him. "Who wants a tummy rub?"

Me. Touch me anywhere. Oh man. It's true what they say
about absence making the heart grow fonder.

I go into the kitchen and put some pad Thai on a plate for
her. "It should still be hot. I timed it for when you'd get here."

She joins me in the kitchen and washes her hands. "I could
get used to this! So attentive and thoughtful, Gage. Careful,
you're going to lose your rep as Mr. Grumps."

I clear my throat. "Thanks."

A few moments later, we settle at the island to eat like
usual, but this time I sit next to her instead of standing across
from her like I usually do to keep a respectful distance.

"So how was your time back in Summerdale?" I know
she's crazy about that town. I'd like her to think about living
here with me in New Jersey, though. We could always visit
Summerdale.

Her blue eyes light up. "Great! You know there's nothing
like home. Probably helps that my brother still lives there,
and everyone I meet is so welcoming. Like I started hanging
with Audrey and her crowd. Do you know Audrey? She actually used to date my brother. She's the librarian in town, but
also active in book club and a bunch of local festivals."

"I might've met her at Paige's wedding."

"Yes, she was there. Audrey and friends were ahead of me
in school, but now that we're adults, the age difference
doesn't matter so much, and we can all hang out."

"I'm older than you by a couple of years, and it seems like
we're the same."

She pats my shoulder. "That's because women mature
light-years faster than men. Anyway, we all went to this

beginner karate class at Drew Robinson's dojo. He's like this majorly hot soldier black-belt dude."

I give her a sideways look for the majorly hot remark, but she continues blithely on. "And Audrey has had a crush on him forever—he just wants to be friends—but then get this, Levi asks her out, perfectly nice guy, and before Audrey can answer, Drew says she's taken. So she gets hopeful like maybe this is beyond friends. Then he invites her to a free beginners karate class."

"That doesn't sound like a date."

"I know, right? But she's hopeful. So she goes and then she gets into it, both for self-defense and the chance to see Drew every week doing his badass thing. We all went to spy for her and let her know our opinion, and the sad truth is, he's nothing but professional."

"Well, he's the teacher, right? Did she expect him to make a move in front of the whole class?"

She rolls her eyes. "He could've talked to her after class any time. But no, he keeps a professional distance. Audrey was really defeated, saying he only saw her as his little sister's friend, but then I thought about the way you look out for Livvie, and I told her not to give up hope. Maybe he wants her to learn self-defense because he cares for her. A lot. I think looking out for someone can sometimes be a way of showing love." She meets my eyes, searching my expression before quickly looking away.

I know nothing about Drew and Audrey as a couple, but I immediately sense a parallel with the professional distance I've kept from Skylar. Time to make my move. "You're right."

She turns to me in surprise, her brows lifting. "I am?"

"Yeah." I shift, hooking my foot on the bottom rung of her chair, my leg between hers. I gaze into her beautiful sky-blue eyes, my heart thumping hard. "You're really smart about people," I murmur, leaning close and cupping her jaw. "You have so many layers, and I want to get to know all of them." I kiss her gently.

She pulls back, searching my expression. "Are we crossing a line here?"

I stiffen. "Maybe I'm not as good at reading people as you are."

"I just want to be sure we're on the same page."

That's exactly what I want, so I blurt everything out, unable to contain it anymore. "I want you here all the time. We can go as slow as you want, but when I look at you, I see a future. You're everything I've ever wanted and everything I didn't know I needed."

She cups my face between her hands. "Yes."

I swallow hard. "Yes, what?"

"I want you too. I've missed you so much these past few days, even though we talked on the phone, and you stopped by to see the mural. It just wasn't the same as when we have time together just the two of us."

"So glad you feel the same way."

She strokes my jaw. "We don't have to dive into something serious, but I like to know you're open to it. For now let's just take it one day at a time."

The last bit of tension leaves my body. She's on board, and she made it so easy. "Sky."

She wraps her arms around my neck and kisses me, hot and eager. I'm on fire. I pull her out of her seat and guide her away from the island.

She breaks the kiss, smiling. "Where are we going?"

I kiss along her neck, nipping and tasting. God, she tastes so fresh and sweet. "Upstairs," I growl in her ear.

"I thought you'd never ask!" She grabs my hand and pulls.

I follow, telling myself to take it slow. Ace gets excited and weaves between our legs. Skylar stumbles, and I grab her before she can fall.

She looks up at me, smiling brightly. "Either Ace is trying to kill me, or he wanted me in your arms."

I scoop her up, cradled in my arms. "There. Now Ace and I both win."

She rubs my chest, smiling. "Do you know how long I've wanted to be carried like this to bed? You're a dream come true."

I crack a smile. "I'll try to live up to that."

"You've already surpassed my expectations."

My chest puffs with pride. "I can't believe I waited so long to do this."

"I'm glad we took the time for true intimacy before getting physical."

"You don't have to gloat about it."

"Gloat about what?"

"Bringing a man to his knees."

"Oh my God, you're killing me here with all your gruff sweetness!" She strokes my jaw. "I can't wait to rip your clothes off."

I chuckle. Seems I got this thing right.

Skylar

Who knew Mr. Grumps could turn into Mr. Sweetness? Though I caught glimpses. Gage sets me down in his room and shuts the door behind us. His dark eyes smolder into mine.

He frames my face with both hands, his words hot against my lips. "God, I missed you."

"Me too."

I'm not sure who moves first, but the kiss is urgent, the expression of so much pent-up desire. Lust fires through my body. He breaks the kiss, his heated gaze on mine as he slowly unbuttons my blouse. His fingers graze my skin, sparks firing everywhere he touches from my collarbone to my stomach. And then he kisses every exposed inch of skin. He's thorough just like he is at work. The thought makes me smile. He undoes my bra and slips it off.

His rough palms skate over my torso, up my sides, and finally to my breasts. He leans down, kissing his way round and round my breast until he reaches the rigid nipple and sucks it into his mouth. My head falls back with the pleasure, my knees going weak.

His arms wrap around me as he kisses me again, backing

me up to the bed and giving me a gentle nudge onto the mattress. He joins me, kissing me as his hand slides down to stroke my thigh through my thin leggings and then run along the inside, slowly moving up, up, up to the heating, throbbing center of me.

I thought he'd be rough and ready, but he's so careful, so thorough. I spread my legs in abandon, a low moan emanating from deep in my throat as he strokes over my center. Back and forth, back and forth. I lift my hips to his rhythm, needing more, much more.

I sit up and strip him out of his clothes, a flurry of movements interrupted only by urgent kisses, but before I can do more than get the briefest of feels of his rounded shoulder with a tribal tattoo, he pushes me to my back and strips me down, peeling off my leggings and panties.

I reach for him, eager to finally join, but he keeps kissing me, stroking me, taking his time as he works his way down my body. I'm hot and tingling from head to toe when he rolls me over and starts all over again, setting sparks of sensation down my spine with every stroke of his calloused fingers, every touch of his lips, his scruff sending delicious shivers through me.

He sends a trail of light kisses back up my spine.

"Gage, I want you."

"I want you more than my next breath."

He rolls me back to face him, and I reach for him. He holds himself up on his forearms, kissing me for so long I melt into the mattress. His hand slips between us, stroking me expertly, and I drop my hold on him, my hands falling limply to the mattress.

He whispers praise in my ear, kissing me as he works magic. My breath comes in short gasps, shocked by the intensity. My body jerks, and I cry out as the release hits hard, an explosion of sensation rocketing through me. He stays with me, letting me ride every last wave until I'm spent.

He kisses me tenderly and leans over to get a condom from the nightstand. I lie there, limp with satisfaction, lazily tracing his tribal tattoo. "I suspected you had more ink on you."

"Did you undress me with your eyes?"

I smile widely. "So many times!"

He positions himself between my legs and slides home slowly, filling me and stealing my breath. He props up on his forearms and kisses my forehead, my nose, my cheeks, and finally my lips. "Beautiful," he whispers.

He moves slow and deep, and I wrap my legs high around his waist, taking him as far as I can. He groans. And then he hits just the right spot, making me crazy. I grab his ass, arching under him, needing more.

"Gage," I manage hoarsely, begging for more.

He thrusts harder and faster, and I pant, along for an exhilarating ride. I throw my head back in ecstasy with a sharp cry. That sets him off, pounding into me, until he lets go with a guttural sound that thrills me, bringing another shock wave of sensation.

He collapses on top of me, pressing his lips to the side of my neck.

I hug him. "I could stay like this forever."

He groans into my neck, vibrating there. Then he rolls to his back.

I curl up next to him.

His big hand comes up to cradle my face. "Was I too rough?"

"Not at all. That was amazing."

He drops his hand and closes his eyes, seeming worn out. "Good."

"I'll turn out the light. You seem tired."

"I helped a friend move today. Worked these muscles."

"Ooh, I would've liked to have seen that. Did you take your shirt off?"

"No, but you can imagine that. Just a minute." He heads to the bathroom, and I stretch out in the cool silk sheets. Wow. Amazing sex with an amazing man.

He slides back into bed, turning onto his stomach. I put an arm around him. "How long until round two?"

He lifts his head. "Seriously?"

"Yes, I've got a lot of built-up horniness where you're concerned, Mr. Sexy."

He drops his head on the pillow, smiling. "Like that better than Mr. Grumps. I'll be good to go in a bit."

I let him sleep, thinking about all that happened here tonight. Gage really opened up to me and basically invited me to live with him permanently. He doesn't seem to know a middle ground between the start of a relationship and permanent, but that's okay. We'll find our way to something that works for both of us.

I realize I haven't been as open as I could be with him. I haven't told anyone about my shameful secret that destroyed my professional reputation. I think I could trust him with it. He respects me and knows I'm not just a flighty free spirit. I have depth.

I must've fallen asleep, because the next thing I know, Gage's spooning me from behind, his erection pressing into my hip, his hand roaming from my stomach to my breast in a heated path. I open my eyes; it's still dark. I'm so turned on already.

"Gage?"

"Good, you're awake." He puts my leg over his, opening me to his exploring hand. Stroking and circling. My eyes roll back in my head. I don't even want to know how he's so good at what he does.

I'm nearly at the edge of release when he stops. "Hey!" I protest.

He pats my bottom. "Just a minute, greedy." And then he pushes my leg up, opening me for his hard thrust. I gasp. Then his hand is back, stroking as he thrusts. I moan loudly. He bites along the cord of my neck, sending electric shocks through my system as he rocks into me, the sensation from his fingers and his relentless thrusts taking over my body. In that moment, he owns me.

I lose myself in an intense spiraling pleasure unlike any I've felt before. My fingers clutch the sheets, my breathing harsh. I cry out, shuddering with my release as fireworks of sensation burst through my body all the way to the ends of my fingers and toes. He keeps going, and I pant helplessly as wave after wave of orgasm crashes over me. He grips my hip tightly as he lets go with a low groan.

We lie there like that, tangled together for long moments, trying to catch our breath. He pulls out and throws an arm around me. Guess he wants me to spend the whole night here with him.

I roll to face him and throw an arm and leg around him. "How long until round three?"

He chuckles. "Greedy little thing."

"I am when it comes to you."

"Me too. You should move into my room. Make it easier on both of us."

"What, you can't work your magic on a twin-size daybed?"

"Magic, huh?" He nuzzles my neck. "I do my best work on a king. You in?"

"Oh, I'm in all right."

"Good," he mumbles. "Cuz I'm *all* in."

My heart squeezes. "Me too."

"Tell me another fact."

This is what we do, share "facts" about ourselves every night at dinner. Of course, facts alone don't do that. True intimacy means sharing from your deepest self.

"I have a secret," I whisper.

He rolls me to my back and stares down at me. I can just make out the angular line of his jaw in the dim light from a nearby streetlight shining through the window. He waits patiently.

"I haven't told anyone this because, I don't know, it's so skeezy it makes me feel dirty." I'm quiet, still uncomfortable saying it out loud.

"Sky, please tell me. My imagination is running wild in the worst way."

"The reason I'm struggling on my own as an interior designer, even though I should've been fine with the money Max gave me from the sale of our family home, is, first, because I spent most of it on a local commercial. Metro New York area commercials cost big bucks."

"You spent all your money on a commercial?"

"No. First I set aside two months' rent, ordered some marketing materials and set up a website, and then I made a professional commercial. It didn't work. Could be reverse ageism, like people don't take me seriously because I'm young. Maybe a more boring commercial that didn't include my face would've helped."

"Why would that make you feel dirty?"

I stare at the ceiling. "It ran for two weeks, and that was the end of my share of the money. Max and Liam would shake their heads over that one."

He cradles my jaw, looking intently at me. "Tell me."

I meet his eyes. "The commercial never stood a chance because my former boss, also an interior designer, destroyed my reputation in the wealthy community where I had made all my contacts. I used to live and work in Greenwich, Connecticut, about forty minutes from Summerdale. That whole area has a lot of luxury homes. They would've seen my commercial since it's in the area." I stare at the ceiling again. "Anyway, my former boss was mad because her husband made a pass at me. I was nice to him, just being my usual friendly self with the best of intentions, but I should've been more careful."

"No. That's not your fault. He made the pass, that's on him."

My eyes get hot, and my throat tight. "I know it, but it still makes me feel awful. Like I can't just be myself because that's inviting the wrong kind of attention in the workplace. That's why I was kinda glad you and I had some distance at work at first. It took the pressure off me trying so hard not to be who I am. How awful is that? I know I shouldn't change for anyone, but after getting burned, I felt like I had to tone everything about me down."

"You're perfect just like you are."

I choke on a laugh. "That's the great sex talking."

"That's me talking. What happened after you turned him down?"

I hug him and let out a breath. "He told me if I told his wife, she'd never believe me. It was my word against his. I was afraid this was going to be an ongoing problem, but then I found out I was getting a windfall of money from the sale of our lake house, so I decided I'd just go out on my own and never have to deal with Brett again. I never told my boss about him making a pass at me. I was scared to set Brett off, and I wasn't sure she'd believe me. But that wasn't the end of it."

Gage's quiet, stroking my hair back from my face.

"After a very confusing time of dead-end marketing, I found out later that he saw the commercial and asked his wife if he could have me as a free pass for his fiftieth-birthday present."

Gage hisses out a breath.

I rush on. "She confronted me and acted like I'd come on to him, encouraging him with this idea, so I told her the truth about how he'd made a pass at me while I still worked for her, but she didn't believe me because I'd waited so long to share. And now she's blacklisted me, warning other wives— who are usually the ones who hire an interior designer—that I'm a threat to their marriages. Me. I've never cheated on anyone in my life, and I'd certainly never break up a marriage."

Gage mutters a curse.

"And so it's been tough to get new clients. Tabitha and Brett are influential with more reach into nearby communities than I realized. I'm basically starting over, cold-calling potential clients, sending out emails, posting interior design articles on social media to get my name out there. And then my condo sold, and I was out of rent money anyway, so here I am."

"Move in with me. Permanently."

My heart pounds. "Gage, we just started seeing each other."

"I was thinking about it anyway. I'm ready for something more, and you need a solid home base to work from."

"That's very kind of you, but—"

"Done deal."

"But—"

"Sky, don't argue with me. Just accept that this is where you belong."

I roll to my side, and he spoons me, holding me tight. "The thought is nice, but I'm not sure we're ready for that."

He kisses my neck. "I want this guy's name in the morning. I'll take care of everything."

"No, I don't want to deal with him. I just need time to rebuild."

"Go to sleep."

"You can't just tell someone to go to sleep."

He rolls on top of me. "Then I guess it's time for round three. Maybe then you'll be tired enough for sleep."

I wrap my arms around him. "You can try to wear me out."

He kisses his way down my body, and my toes curl. *Yes, yes, yes.*

15

Gage

When I wake the next morning, I'm still pissed about Skylar's confession. I sit up in bed and rub my jaw. That anyone could make her feel ashamed for something that wasn't her fault, it's plain wrong. I look over at her sleeping on her side, her silky hair spread across the pillow, looking like an angel. No way I'm letting this stand.

I go downstairs to take care of Ace, get the coffeemaker going, and then I go upstairs for a shower. I'm half-dressed, jeans on, when Skylar wakes, stretching like a cat.

"Good morning," she says cheerfully.

"Wow, you're that sunny in the morning without coffee."

She smiles and opens her arms to me. "I had a very good night."

I sit next to her on the bed and hug her. And then I can't help but kiss her, stroking her hair back and cradling her jaw. She's precious, and I'll do my damndest to protect her.

She pulls back. "Is something wrong?"

"I can't stop thinking about what you said last night about your former boss and her sleazy husband."

"Yes, well, I'm working on ways around it."

"It's wrong, and I'm going to make it right."

"Gage, no. This is my problem. I didn't tell you so you'd rescue me."

"It's not right what either one of them did. He never should've hit on you, and she shouldn't have blacklisted you because he had the stupid idea to ask for you as a birthday present. What kind of sicko does that?"

"A privileged rich man used to getting his way."

My fists clench. "Not anymore."

"But what will confronting them do? If I confront him, he'll probably see it as encouragement that I sought him out. If I confront her, she's not going to suddenly sing my praises to her contacts. The damage is done."

"I'm fixing this. I can't just stand by and do nothing."

She rubs my shoulder. "So I have to work a little harder to find new clients instead of picking off the ready-made network I had. That's not the worst thing. This way my ex-boss and I won't be stepping on each other's toes, bidding in the same territory."

"But you haven't found work. You're broke."

She leaps out of bed and grabs her clothes from the floor. "Thanks for the cold splash of reality. Not that I needed it. I told you I'm working on it." She rushes to the bathroom.

I rest my elbows on my knees. If I hadn't offered her a place to live, she'd be homeless. Okay, she could stay at the studio apartment behind her brother Max's house, but I don't like that option either. Once my job is finished on Spencer and Paige's home renovation, I won't be in Summerdale anymore. I've already got several jobs lined up here in New Jersey. And the truth is, I don't want her so far from me. I want her to live here and have as many wealthy clients as she can handle. She deserves that. This problem ends now.

I pull on a T-shirt and knock on the bathroom door.

"Come in," she says.

I open the door and see her brushing her teeth at the sink. "Found an extra toothbrush in the drawer."

"That's where I keep them." I find myself smiling. I love seeing her at home in my bathroom. She's wearing just her blouse and lacy blue panties. Bare feet.

Then I remember my purpose. "What's the name of the interior design firm you used to work for?"

She holds up a palm in the universal stop sign and rinses. After she dries her mouth with a hand towel, she gives me a squinty-eyed look. "I told you I'm working around it. The damage is done, and there's no point in dredging up the past. Besides, what're you going to do, tell them off? That's not going to help anything."

More like kick this guy's ass, but she doesn't need to know that. "I thought we shared stuff. Isn't that how we have that intimacy you told me about?"

She rolls her eyes. "Intimacy is when two people become close, and we are close. I shared my secret with you, but that doesn't mean you have to do anything about it. I'm happy to hear your secrets and be a great listener for you too."

"I don't have any secrets. I already told you everything you need to know."

"So now everything's out in the open. Fantastic."

"Yes, but…" I trail off as she whips her blouse off and tosses it at me. She turns the shower on, bending toward it in her skimpy blue panties.

My mouth goes dry. "Do you still wear the Wonder Woman panties?"

She looks at me over her shoulder. "Of course. Every laundry day they give me a much-needed morale boost to make the world a better place with beautiful design that brings comfort and pleasure."

I wrap my arms around her from behind. "You can make my world a better place." I kiss her neck and tug her panties down.

She turns in my arms, giving me a slow sexy smile. "Care to join me?"

I yank my shirt off. "Yes."

"Okay, but you have to drop this thing with my ex-boss and let me handle it."

I unbutton my jeans, my gaze eating her up. There's not much I'd deny her at a moment like this. "Okay, you handle it, but keep me in the loop. I want to know what you do and what the result is."

She steps into the shower. "Very good. I'm waiting for you, my sexy protector."

I strip the rest of my clothes and join her, wrapping my arms around her and kissing her long and deep. "Sexy protector, I like that."

"I like it too. You make me feel safe. Speaking of safety, did you happen to bring a condom?"

"I plan on working around that."

"Oh?"

I kiss her luscious mouth and then work my way down her body, stopping on my knees to taste her. She moans loudly, turning me on even more, and then she rocks her hips to my rhythm as I bring her to the ultimate pleasure. I watch as she comes apart, her head tilting back, her body arching in ecstasy.

I stand, and she hangs onto me heavily. "My legs are shaking."

"Good."

"I still need to wash."

"I'll do it." I take my time with the washcloth, teasing and cleaning her at the same time. She whimpers and writhes against me. "Gage, I need you so bad."

Lust surges through me. "Hang on."

I rinse her, turn off the water, and dry us both before carrying her back to bed. She sighs as her back sinks into the mattress, and spreads her legs wide for me.

Jesus. There's nothing I wouldn't do for this woman. I swear I'll make everything right in her world just like she's done for me.

I grab a condom, roll it on, and join her, entwining our fingers together.

"Ahhh, yess," she hisses out.

I kiss her again and again, slowly rocking into her until I finally come up for air. I gaze into her eyes reflecting dazed wonder, amping up the intensity. There's a connection here unlike any I've ever felt.

She pulls me toward her roughly, arching her hips. I speed up, hard and fast, driving into her until I feel her go off, the rhythmic clasping sending me over with her in an explosive orgasm.

After I catch my breath, I nuzzle her neck. "I'm going to give the world to you."

"You know, the first time I met you, I didn't like you very much." I can hear the smile in her voice.

I lift my head, smiling. "No, say it isn't so."

She nods vigorously. "It's true."

"What about the second time?"

"Nope."

"Third?"

She crinkles her nose. "A little bit."

"Only a little?"

"It turned into a lot when I saw how sweet you were with Ace, cuddling him on the sofa. Also, the care you take with your sister."

"So my offering to let you live here and give you a job didn't make you like me a whole hell of a lot more?"

She hugs me. "Maybe. I really fell when you turned sweet and tender. I know you're making an extra effort just for me."

"You're the only one I ever wanted to make an effort for."

"Oh, Gage!"

She kisses me all over my face, and I can't stop smiling.

∼

Skylar

After more than one intense conversation with Gage over letting me handle my boss problem, I finally decide to meet with Tabitha. It's been six months since her husband requested me as his birthday gift, and I'd like to at least make peace with her. We're both professionals, and I'd appreciate it if she'd stop bad-mouthing me.

It's Friday morning, and we're meeting at a coffee shop in Greenwich, close to her design firm. She didn't want to meet me at work, which is fine by me since I don't want my former coworkers to witness our talk. Tabitha was my first boss out of college, and for a long time, I looked up to her as a mentor. She often let me come up with original design ideas and put together presentations on my own. Even if she didn't compliment me in front of clients, she always did praise me in private, letting me know she appreciated my creative contribution.

I find her sitting in a quiet corner with coffee already. She's busy with her phone, so I go to place an order for herbal tea and join her a few moments later.

"Hi, Tabitha, thanks for taking the time to meet with me."

She doesn't smile. "I don't have long. What's this about?"

"I know you're not happy with me right now because you think I'm interested in Brett, but nothing could be farther from the truth. He came on to me, and I turned him down. That was the end of it like I told you before. And then I guess he saw my commercial and thought about me again, but I never had any contact with him in between, I swear."

She glares at me. "I find that hard to believe."

"Okay, well, I have nothing to gain by lying. And I'd really appreciate it if you'd stop bad-mouthing me to potential clients. You know how crucial word-of-mouth is in this business. I'm not trying to steal your clients, and I'm certainly not trying to steal your husband. I would never break up a marriage." At her skeptical expression, I blurt, "Seriously! He's twice my age, married, and smells like my grandpa's aftershave."

"Oh geez." Her lips twitch, and she sets down her coffee. I can't tell if she's about to laugh or cry.

"Tabitha?"

She lets out a short laugh and wipes her eyes. Her nose is red. "I guess Brett's not the catch he thinks he is."

"Not at all. Besides that undeniable fact, I respect you so much as a designer, a boss, and a friend. I would never do anything to hurt you."

She breaks down, tears leaking out of her eyes. I pass her a napkin since I don't have tissues.

"I'm sorry," she says in between small sobs. "I never

should've...I took it out on you. Brett's had a wandering eye for years, and I just tried to ignore it. But then when he asked for a pass to go for you as a fiftieth-birthday gift, I just lost it. I thought it must be something real if he's asking permission instead of going behind my back."

"Do people really do that?"

"We've been married twenty-eight years. It's easy to fall into a routine, so busy with work and the kids. Course it's mostly me keeping our family running." She blows her nose on the napkin. "We certainly wouldn't be the first with an open marriage."

I try not to cringe. "I can't imagine my boyfriend ever wanting an open relationship. He's very loyal and protective. He'd probably kill any rival for trying."

Fresh tears burst out of her.

"Not literally. Maybe he'd try to kick their ass." *And succeed. He's a strong powerful man who works those muscles daily.* I relax a little, thinking of Gage and how wonderful it feels to be held in his firm embrace.

"I don't want an open relationship!" Tabitha cries.

I trace a circle on the table, giving her a moment.

She fishes a tissue from her purse, wipes her eyes, and blows her nose. "Sorry."

"It's okay."

She stuffs her phone and tissue back in her purse. "I should go. I'm making a scene here."

"Wait! Can you please tell people I'm not a husband stealer? I've been having trouble picking up new clients."

She frowns. "Skylar, I can't admit my husband humiliated me this way. It has to seem like your fault."

I stiffen. "No, it doesn't."

She gives me an assessing look. "I'll give you some money to tide you over. How much would you like?"

"I'm not taking your money. This is about my reputation."

She stands. "I'm afraid there isn't much more I can do."

I stand too. "You could fix the damage you did to my reputation."

She pulls her wallet out and throws a couple of hundred-dollar bills on the table. "Best I can do when you're so inflexible. Really, Skylar, you need to learn to play ball."

She puts sunglasses on to cover her red eyes and strides toward the door.

I grab the money and shake it at her back as she walks away. "This money is better spent on a divorce lawyer!"

She hurries away.

I exhale sharply. Then I go to the counter and put the money in the tip jar. I can't even with some people.

I go back for my tea and head out the door. I don't see her out here. She must've left in a hurry. At least I know one thing for sure. I made the right move leaving her design firm. Who knows how she might've sabotaged me if she were still my boss!

16

Gage

It's dinnertime, and Skylar shares her big news as soon as we sit at my new rectangular wooden kitchen table with take-out Italian. She likes to sit close to me, adjacent to the head of the table. Ace sits a short distance away so he can stare at me as I eat.

"I took care of it," she says proudly. "I met with my former boss, told her to correct the damage she's done, and she finally saw the truth about her husband."

"So what is she doing for you?"

She takes a long drink of water. "The important thing is, I finally got to say what was weighing so heavily on my mind. Now I feel lighter." She goes back to her penne alla vodka.

I put a hand on her arm, leaning close. "What exactly do you get as compensation for the damage she did to your reputation?"

"She offered money, but I don't want her money. I told her to use it on a divorce lawyer."

"That *almost* sounds like you got angry." She's too damn nice.

"I told you it was mostly in the past. I just wanted her to know the truth."

"Not good enough."

She shakes her head and stabs a piece of penne. "I can't force her to say good things about me. At least now maybe she'll stop saying bad things about me."

"Maybe isn't good enough."

"It's not like I'm going to work in Greenwich anyway. Just like many new entrepreneurs, it takes time to get things off the ground. I'll find my clients soon, I'm sure."

I clamp my mouth shut. Can I confront this asshole who came on to her now? I don't want her to confront him, that's for sure. I said I'd let her handle the problem. She tried, but it didn't fix the problem; therefore, it's up to me.

She leans close, smiling. "Now you share something about you."

"My top favorite moments in Giants football are as follows—"

"Not factoids about sporting events I know nothing about. Share from the heart. Did you have a dog growing up?"

"I did, but then after Rusty died, Mom said we couldn't afford another one. She was right."

She gives me a hug. "I'm glad you have Ace now."

"Me too. And I'm glad I have you."

She gives my cheek a pat. "So sweet! I had no idea there was anything sweet hiding under that grumpy exterior."

"I'm not grumpy. I'm just serious at work."

"And at home, but you're starting to lighten up. Thanks to me."

"No doubt."

She smiles and goes back to eating.

And there's no doubt I'm going to find out this bastard's name and make him pay for all the damage he and his wife did to a woman who deserves nothing but the best.

The next morning I track down the asshole at his country club just as he's leaving from a Saturday morning tee time. It wasn't hard to find him. Skylar's website lists projects from her former design firm. I got her former boss's name and then her husband from there. A quick Google search and social media told me plenty. Brett's a middle-aged guy with thinning brown hair and a paunch, who loves golf and a good whiskey. He runs his own hedge fund.

"Brett, can we talk for a minute?"

He stares at me and then gives me a blank smile. "I seem to be at a loss here. I don't remember your name."

"That's because we've never met, but you know a friend of mine, Skylar Bellamy. She used to work for your wife."

He smiles blandly. "Oh yeah, Skylar. Nice young woman. Hard worker, according to my wife."

"She was working nonstop until your wife trashed her reputation." I lean close for the kill. "And why would your wife do that?"

His expression turns blank. "I'm sure you're wrong. Tabitha's a professional."

"Unfortunately, it's true. All because you came on to Skylar and asked your wife for a fiftieth-birthday pass." I jab him in the chest. "Seriously fucked up, Brett. So Tabitha takes it out on Skylar, blaming her and spreading the word that she's the kind to steal your husband, which means no one wants her in their home. She can't line up enough work because of the damage that you and your wife did." I jab him in the chest again and say loud enough for everyone in town to hear, "To an innocent, hardworking, talented professional."

He glances around and pulls at the collar of his designer polo shirt. "I don't know what you want me to do about it. I haven't seen Skylar since she went out on her own."

"It's your fault this whole thing blew up in her face. Fix it. Refer her to all your rich friends."

"I can't do that. Tabitha and I have the same friends, and it seems they believe Skylar's a marriage wrecker. I had no idea Tabitha took my request so hard. She never mentioned it again."

I exhale sharply. "Think real hard, Brett. How else can you make this right for Skylar? She's broke. A talented interior designer like her with no clients and no income. What can you do?"

I know Sky said she doesn't want their money, but I'm getting it to her one way or another. It's the only way to ensure she has a stable foundation to move forward.

He nods like a bobblehead. "I'll write her a check." He pats his pockets. "I don't have my checkbook with me."

"Have you heard of online banking?"

He grimaces. "I'm afraid I'm old school in that regard."

"Then let's take a ride to find that checkbook."

He swallows audibly. "I'll call the cops if you lay a hand on me."

"You deserve a good ass kicking, but I'll settle for making this right with Skylar."

"Are you two together?"

"How perceptive you are, Brett. Hard to believe how majorly you fucked everything up with your selfish cheating ways. And now that I think about it, you need to apologize to Skylar."

"I don't have her number."

I pull out my phone and call Skylar. "Hello!" she answers cheerfully. "Where'd you get off to so early this morning?"

"I have someone here who wants to talk to you." I hand him the phone.

"Hi, Skylar, it's, uh, Brett, Tabitha's husband." He glances at me before walking a distance away. I follow him just as he says, "Your boyfriend is crazy. He stalked me at the country club, and now he's going to my house and forcing a check out of me."

I grab him by the collar and pull him close. "Tell her the truth and apologize."

His eyes get huge. "I'm sorry for any trouble I caused, Skylar. I'm writing a check to get you back on your feet."

I shake him and then drop my hold on him. He drops my phone in the process.

I scoop it up. "You still there?" I follow Brett to a cherry red Ferrari that probably costs a fortune.

"Gage, what are you doing?" Skylar asks quietly.

"I'll explain later." I hang up and jerk my head toward Brett's car. "Let's go."

He unlocks it, and I get in the passenger side. My phone rings again. Skylar. I put it on silent mode and let it go to voicemail. She'll thank me once I get this score settled. No one messes with my woman.

~

Skylar

I pace the front hallway of Gage's home, furious with him for butting into my life. I told him I'd take care of it, he said he would let me handle it, yet he broke his promise. He doesn't see me as capable, just like my family. I've learned to look before I leap now. I take a moment to think things through.

*Grr...*He was completely in the wrong, and the fact that he doesn't trust me to deal with my own life only says I can expect more of the same from him. He'll say he believes in me and then go off and take care of my problems his way. Who knows what he did to Brett? Beat him up? Humiliate him in front of his country club friends? How is that helping? Brett will tell Tabitha everything, and it'll just add fuel to the fire. I'll be the homewrecker designer with a crazy boyfriend who goes after people.

I stop pacing as a stab of worry hits me. What if Brett and Tabitha start trashing Gage's reputation too? What if Brett calls the police? I can only pray they don't have reach in New Jersey. I know that's where most of Gage's clients are, including his next projects.

Ace stares at me from the end of the hallway.

I throw my hands up and tell Ace all my troubles. "Why am I so worried about him? I'm the one in a bad spot, and he's making it worse! I can't live with this man even one more day."

Ace cocks his head to the side in confusion.

I march upstairs and start packing. At least my work here is done. I was only sticking around because I thought we had something special. Turns out we don't.

I finish packing and then flop down on the bed. I'm in

Gage's room, which was starting to feel like my room too. My stuff was in the closet. I put up curtains and a few framed art prints and changed the bedding to a soothing blue comforter. I was thinking of doing a special paint technique on the walls for shades of light blue. Hot tears sting my eyes. I can't leave until Gage gets here. I need to tell him face-to-face exactly why I'm leaving.

I'm so mad!

And sad too. I curl on my side. And heartbroken. I hear a snuffling sound and find Ace standing with his front paws on the mattress. "C'mere, Ace. I'm going to miss your funny little face." I pull him up on the bed with me, and he cuddles against my side. I stroke his fur, telling myself I'm doing the right thing. There's no justification for what Gage did. I'll hear him out, but I doubt there's any good reason for butting in and certainly not for acting like a crazy man, stalking Brett and then forcing him to write a check.

I told Tabitha I wouldn't take her money, and now Brett's giving me that same money. I take a deep calming breath and think it through. It's not like Brett can't afford it, and he was the one who caused all these problems. Even though what I really want to do is rip that check to pieces, I won't. It's okay to take his money since he's the problem. I have only one project on the horizon—Spencer and Paige's home renovation —and now that I'm planning on moving out of Gage's place, I'll be homeless once again. Sure, I can go back to Max's place, but soon I'll have to explain my utter failure both with my job and with the windfall he gave me from our family home.

And I still miss that house! Gone forever. *Demolished.* I cry in earnest then. Ace licks my face, giving me kisses and clearing some of the tears. I laugh through my tears. "You're such a love bug."

I sit up, thinking more clearly now. I'm going to be practical and use that money for rent on an apartment, and any left over will go toward savings. I don't want to blow it on expensive marketing efforts. Maybe I should start over in Summerdale. There's not any wealthy clients there, except for Wyatt Winters, who already renovated and decorated his home, but people know me and trust me. My sister-in-law Brooke is a residential architect, and she did offer to refer people my way. She volunteered Wyatt's help too, but I hadn't wanted to bother him while he was dealing with a newborn screamer.

I go down the hall to my home office and settle on the daybed with my laptop, looking over the portfolio on my website. I can add the comfortable interior design I did at Gage's house to attract locals who might not want the elegant look of my previous projects with lots of silk and crystal. I have the inn and restaurant under commercial projects. Then there's my new mural option. I have two projects to show for it. Maybe something will come of that too. All is not lost. I can do this.

"Why the hell are your suitcases packed?" Gage barks from the doorway, startling me.

Adrenaline races through me. I lift my chin. "You crossed the line. Not cool, Gage. I told you I'd handle it, and you went behind my back and probably made a worse mess of things. What were you thinking stalking Brett at his country club and forcing him to write a check?"

"That's his version of things. I tracked him down and demanded he make things right. He knew what he had to do. It's the only thing that gets you back on your feet. Compensate you for your lack of clients, which is through no fault of your own." He pulls a check from his back pocket and hands it to me. "That should tide you over for at least a year."

"A year," I whisper. I look down at a check with many more zeroes than I expected. Holy shit. One hundred thousand dollars. I could pay off my student loan *completely*, move into my own apartment, *and* still have leftover money to stash in savings.

He sits next to me. "It's good, right?" he says proudly.

I carefully fold the check and tuck it into my trouser pocket. "Did you threaten him? Force his hand?"

He scowls. "What kind of person do you think I am? I didn't hold him at gunpoint. I just told him to make it right. Then I thanked him and told him I hoped never to see him again and not to contact you, which he was happy to agree to. I don't see how there's anything wrong with that. In fact, you should've done the same when it first happened."

I suppress a shudder. "I never wanted to see him again. And I certainly wasn't going to put myself at risk by being alone with him. You think he would've written me a check if I'd asked? He'd probably assume I wanted a paid sex arrangement."

He crosses his arms. "That's why you need me."

"No, not like this. I'm sorry, but I can't be with someone who doesn't believe in my abilities."

His voice softens. "Of course I believe in your abilities. You're an amazing artist. I show your murals to everyone."

"And I appreciate that, but you also went behind my back and took over my problem that I told you I'd already dealt with."

"It wasn't dealt with. You were still broke with no clients. Now you can have the fresh start you need."

"And what will my ex-boss say about me now? She'll be even more furious that her husband wrote me this huge check."

"He took it from an account she doesn't know about. I asked him about that, trying to minimize collateral damage."

I shake my head. "That is one screwed-up marriage."

"Be glad you're free of them."

I sigh. "It still doesn't change the fact that you took over my problem after I told you I could handle it."

"But you couldn't handle it."

"Yes, I can."

"I'm still waiting for my thank-you."

I shoot him a pointed look and power down my laptop before slipping it into its case.

"This is good!" he exclaims. "You don't have to worry, and you have time to really make a go of your business."

I slowly stand. "I'm sorry. It's just not going to work out. I'm moving back to Max's cottage until I can find a place of my own."

He stands, his expression pained. "Sky, don't go. Please."

I hug him, my eyes hot. "Bye."

I gather my things and head to his bedroom for my suitcases.

"You're ungrateful!" he yells, appearing in his bedroom a moment later.

I close my eyes and take a deep breath before facing him. "I appreciate you letting me stay here and giving me a job. I hope you like the results."

He watches from the doorway as I take one last look around. "If I forgot anything, you can give it to me at Spencer and Paige's house. I'll see you there for work in a week."

I walk out on wooden legs, my heart breaking, a lump of emotion lodged in my throat. I'm nearly at the front door when he calls to me from the top of the stairs.

"This is exactly why I didn't want to get involved in the first place! Now it's a mess, and I'll have to see you at work."

"Life's messy, Gage."

"I don't like a mess. I'll come in early so we don't have to see each other."

Ace barks at me from the top of the stairs, joining his owner's outrage.

Tears swim in front of my eyes, but I force myself to walk out the door. Time for that fresh start.

17

Gage

Despite my plan to avoid Skylar in the case of a fallout, it only took twenty-four hours of misery to realize I can't bear the thought of never seeing her again. I finagled the schedule to get Skylar in on Monday morning for work at Spencer and Paige's house. I couldn't wait even a week to see her. My schedule aligns with hers. We can't be done yet. I did the right thing. I helped her.

The moment she walks in, I confront her with my well-reasoned argument for why she should come back to my house. "You never finished the job at my house. Our agreement was you live there while you work on my place. It's not finished."

She sighs. "It *is* finished. Everything we discussed is in place."

"What about a finished basement? You said you could make the man cave nicer than just a card table and a bar. That could be a big selling point."

"Gage, can you just let me work here? I have a lot to do. Spencer and Paige are tired of people coming in and out of their house. Paige wants to feather her nest."

My brows scrunch together. "I don't know what that means."

"She wants to do stuff to get her house ready for the baby. It's like a maternal energy. So if you really want me to do more work for you, let me finish up here, and we'll talk. But I'm not moving in again. I'll commute from wherever I land."

"Where are you moving?"

"I'm going to look for my own place in Summerdale. I'm hoping to build a client base here. I like making people's homes more comfortable, and maybe some of them will let me paint a mural too. It's not Greenwich, but it suits my taste better anyway."

"*Let* you paint a mural? They should pay you for your talent."

"Thank you." And then she walks away.

My chest aches fiercely. I hate this.

"Sky, hold up." I catch up with her by the stairs. "I have a question about the master bath. Paige wants a different color palette."

She lifts a hand. "Under control." Then she goes upstairs.

My crew already finished upstairs, which is why I'm down here. All I have left to do is an enclosed sun porch out back. Then I'll never see Skylar again. My gut churns. I'll hire her for more stuff. There's always more you can do to a house. I can buy a new house and have her do stuff there.

And then what? You can't keep hiring her just to keep her close.

Fucking hell. I miss her. She's right upstairs, yet she feels a million miles away.

I stalk to the back of the house where two guys on crew are waiting.

"Done talking to your girlfriend?" one guy asks.

"Don't mention her name to me again."

"Uh-oh."

"Shut up."

Then I get to work, pushing thoughts of Sky from my mind. In time she'll appreciate how much I helped her, wringing that check out of sleazy Brett. My spirits lift as a thought occurs that finally feels right. She'll come back to me when she realizes how much better off she is because of me. I'll be gracious and accept her back no questions asked.

Skylar

Only two and a half weeks later, my work on Spencer and Paige's house is complete. I've told everyone that I'm staying in Summerdale and to keep me in mind for murals as well as interior design work. Brooke has a couple of meetings set up for me with her residential architectural clients, and Max was so thrilled I'd be staying in town he didn't question why I'm no longer working for wealthy clients in Greenwich. Maybe Brooke convinced him I know what I'm doing with my business plan and marketing efforts. Besides, I have a built-in network here. I couldn't ask for anything more.

Well, except for Gage to show up with a huge apology and swear he'll never take over my life again and believes in me wholeheartedly. I shake my head. Like that would ever happen. I miss him, and it's been really hard. I think of him often, even texted him a few times, but then I deleted the texts without sending. Nothing's changed. He still believes he's in the right and I should be grateful for his interference. I guess you could say I liked the results—the money to get me back on my feet—but not the method.

Maybe if he'd included me in the venture, I wouldn't have felt so betrayed. Truth is, I thought I wanted a knight in shining armor, but what I really want is a partner. Someone on my team, not someone to swoop in and rescue me.

It's a bright sunny April day as I walk over to the Inn at Lover's Lane. I'm still at Max's cottage, waiting for a rental to open up. I actually found a place, the apartment over Summerdale Sweets. I'm taking over Sloane and Caleb's apartment in two months when they move into a house they just bought in town.

Anyway, I'm heading to the inn for an interview with *Leisure Travel* magazine in advance of their elopement wedding coverage this summer. They like to do some of their research ahead of time. Brooke and Paige were kind enough to include me in the hopes that my mural could be featured in the magazine.

There's a bunch of cars parked out front and a Harley motorcycle. Wow. Looks like a crowd. I thought it would just be a reporter and journalist. Paige lives next door, and Brooke could just walk over from down the street.

I ring the doorbell of the inn and then let myself in the front door with my key. Paige let me keep the key since I've worked with them for so long. She credits me for creating a warm ambiance at the inn and at Spencer's, the restaurant next door.

Paige meets me in the living room. "Hi!" She hugs me.

"How's the baby?"

She smiles and rubs her stomach. "I'm almost four months. Can you see the bump?" She smooths her maroon cotton shirt down, but her stomach still looks flat.

"Uh, not too much."

She thrusts her stomach out and then turns sideways. "Look, there's a definite rounding."

"Oh, yeah, I see it now. So cool!" *Barely there.*

She beams. "Right? Everyone's out back at the wedding pergola. I just stopped inside to grab our wedding photo album to show what the outside looks like fully decorated." She turns and walks toward the back door.

I follow. "Why're there so many cars out front?"

"It's the reporter, a photographer, an assistant, and Levi stopped by to pick up his check, and they wanted to talk to him too since he's our officiant so often. Oh, and our elopement bride is here. She's Kayla's friend from work, so Kayla met her here to show her around." Kayla is her younger sister.

I step out on the deck with her. "No groom?"

"He's content to let the bride pick out everything. Too busy with work."

"On a Saturday?"

"He's one of those research scientists who spends all his time at the lab." She lowers her voice. "Easier for us. All we have to do is please the bride."

I join everyone at the pergola, and Paige hands her photo album to the reporter, a young red-haired guy wearing a beige button-down shirt with dark gray trousers and leather shoes. The photographer, a brunette woman with her hair in a sophisticated twist wearing a purple wrap dress, leans close to look at the photo album with him. Very stylish these two.

Paige points out the bride to me in a whisper.

"What kind of work do you do?" Levi asks the bride with a warm smile. She's cute with dark brown hair in a messy bun, glowing olive skin, and dark brown eyes magnified by large black-framed glasses with a smudged fingerprint on them. Her fashion sense is nerdy scientist—a faded T-shirt with jeans so old they're white in places.

Hold on. Is that Wonder Woman on her faded T-shirt? *Hell yeah. Soul sisters.* I'm about to compliment her shirt when I notice her gaze is locked on Levi in an intense stare, like she just discovered a soul connection. Or maybe Levi's looking at her like that, and she's staring back wondering why.

She starts to speak and then coughs to clear her throat before answering Levi's question about her work. "I'm in the biostatistics department with Kayla at a pharmaceutical company. We ensure the data for new drugs and treatments is analyzed properly."

He steps closer, a hint of flirtiness to his voice. "Sounds like important work. I'm the mayor, fourth-generation Summerdale resident. Anything you need while you're here, let me know."

Doesn't he know she's the bride?

She blushes and goes to tuck her hair behind her ears, but it's already pulled up in a bun. "Thank you. That's kind of you. I just moved here in a house only one street over from the lake. If I use my telescope, I can see the water from my back deck."

"Postcard quality," he says warmly. "We haven't been introduced. I'm Levi—"

Kayla pipes up. "Sorry, there's been no time for proper introductions. Galena, this is Levi Appleton. Levi, this is my good friend Galena Torres soon-to-be *Mrs.* Galena Rutkowski."

Subtle way of getting the message across.

Levi stops smiling, his expression quickly changing to neutral friendly territory. "Nice to meet you."

"I won't be taking his name," Galena says to Kayla. "I'm known professionally as Galena Torres. It's not necessary to have the same last name when you don't plan to have children."

"I guess I'll see you this June," Levi says. "I'm the officiant for the weddings here unless you have someone else you'd like to use."

"No, you'll do fine," Galena says. "Simple and no fuss is why I'm here."

Levi inclines his head and walks off.

She doesn't sound like a very enthusiastic bride, though if she were, it would suck to have a fiancé who didn't share in that enthusiasm.

A few moments later, the roar of a Harley sounds in the background. Guess that sweet ride was Levi's. Seems our upstanding mayor has a wild side.

The reporter claps. "I like what I see. Galena, would you mind if we talked to you and your fiancé in advance of the big day?"

"You can talk to me now. You won't see my fiancé until the wedding day. He's much too busy. He wasn't too keen on being featured, but I asked him as a favor to Kayla and by extension her sisters."

Kayla throws an arm around Galena and gives her a squeeze. "My honorary sister."

Galena smiles shyly. "Yes. We have a lot in common with work and our family background."

Kayla smiles. "Galena is the youngest in her family and the smartest. Just like me."

Paige laughs.

"Seriously, Kayla," Brooke says, glancing at the reporter. They're her two older sisters.

"What? Are we denying I inherited Dad's mathematical brilliance?" Kayla asks with wide innocent eyes.

Brooke hitches a thumb toward Paige. "So we got the scraps in the gene pool?"

"No," Kayla says, nodding. She elbows Galena, who bites back a smile.

"Get outta here," Paige says.

"Kidding!" Kayla says, hugging both her sisters at the same time.

After they break apart, the reporter pulls Galena aside to talk.

"You'll go next," Paige says to me, indicating the reporter guy. "They loved the mural on the tour, so it'll be an easy interview."

I wait for my turn and then go inside with the reporter and photographer for pictures with my mural. I'm a little embarrassed I didn't glam up for the occasion. I didn't realize I'd be in any of the pictures. I'm wearing a long pink tunic with gray leggings and flats. My hair is down, and I've got on pink lip gloss. That's it.

"Tell us about your process," the reporter says.

I spy the historic picture on the dining table and pick it up. "Here's the original picture I worked from. The inn used to be a Dutch farmhouse that was originally built in the 1700s. They added on here on the side around nineteen twenty. I took a little artistic liberty and imagined what it might've looked like on a summer day just as visitors are arriving."

"Phenomenal," the photographer says. "Who did you study with?"

"Oh, uh, nobody. This is just something I enjoy doing in my spare time. I made a mural in my bedroom growing up, and then I did one for a client." I pull my phone out to show them the mural from Gage's house. Bittersweet memories swamp me, remembering all the dinners we shared, the way he shared a fact every night in an effort to discover intimacy with me. My throat nearly closes with emotion.

Her brows shoot up. "No training. Interesting. Did you work from a picture for this piece as well?"

I swallow over the lump in my throat. "This is actually the view I grew up with of Lake Summerdale. This client let me choose a subject of my choice, so I picked my favorite place in the world."

They exchange a look before the reporter says, "If you're open to doing work in an office, I'd love to recommend you to my boss for a mural. It would be so inspirational for us. Maybe a New England scene in the fall in vibrant color like you did here." He indicates Gage's mural.

"Or spring," the photographer says, framing a mural in the air. "When everything comes into bloom."

"Aren't you in the city?" I ask.

They nod.

"I bet I could paint Central Park in one of your favorite seasons or all seasons with one in each quadrant. I could sketch out a few ideas and send them over to you."

The reporter fishes a business card from his pocket and hands it to me. "Can't wait to see what you come up with."

I smile, pleased I'm already finding new work and for a national magazine too.

Paige joins us. "I can vouch for her with the big guy." She turns to me. "I know the owner of the media company that runs *Leisure Travel*."

I bounce on the balls of my feet. "Thank you so much. I appreciate the opportunity."

I leave shortly after that, walking back to my studio apartment, thinking of Gage. He's the one who encouraged me to paint again, even bringing me a huge gift bag of art supplies. If it weren't for him, I wouldn't have rediscovered this well of creativity that I'm so jazzed about. It could be a good sideline, or even a whole new career for me, one that feeds my soul.

Either way, I owe it all to him. Gage changed my life for the better. I should try to connect with him again.

No, he was the one who crossed the line; he's the one who needs to make things right. I can't keep letting people off the hook. I learned that lesson the hard way with Tabitha.

18

_____

Gage

My work here in Summerdale is done, but I show up on a Saturday for Spring Fling, not to be confused with Spring Carnival in May. Apparently, this April weekend's festival is just to keep kids busy during spring break. I'm hoping to run into Skylar. She hasn't returned any of my phone calls, but when I texted her a happy birthday note earlier this week, she responded with a cheerful, "Thank you!" That's all it took to give me a drop of hope. Pathetic.

It's been three weeks since she moved out of my house, telling me goodbye, and I want her back. I still don't know how to make that happen. Wouldn't any decent boyfriend stand up for their woman and make things right? My gut says that was the way to go. Her life was chaos, and I brought it back to order. That's what I do. What the hell is wrong with her not to appreciate that?

I walk around the main fairground, a large piece of grassy land next to the Presbyterian church, as kids chase each other and zip over to the bouncy house. The smell of cooking meat reaches me, and my stomach growls. I haven't been eating much lately, haven't been sleeping much either. I get in line at a white tent where The Horseman Inn is cooking up burgers, hot dogs, and veggie burgers.

Someone pokes me in the back. "Hello, Gage, are you feeling more welcome in town?"

I turn to see Mrs. Ellis, the woman who runs the welcoming committee and asks too many personal questions. Skylar says everyone calls her General Joan behind her back. "Guess so. Finished my job here, yet I came back on the weekend." I don't mention Skylar. My heart is too heavy to say her name without giving away too much.

"Any improvement in your work relationship with Skylar?" Mrs. Ellis asks.

There's a loaded question.

"Everything's fine. Besides, our project's finished."

"Do you plan to see her again?"

I look away. *I saw her plenty, and now I'm not sure she wants to see me.*

She pats my arm. "I can see in your eyes you're in pain. You love her."

Yup. Doesn't change anything. I glance around, looking for signs of Skylar, but she's nowhere to be found. I even spot the women she hangs out with—Audrey and friends—but she's not with them.

"Well?" Mrs. Ellis asks.

"Doesn't matter how I feel."

She jabs me in the gut. "Course it matters."

"Next!" the cashier says.

I move up and place my order, and then I ask Mrs. Ellis what she'd like and pay for hers too.

She smiles. "Thank you, that was very gentlemanly of you."

"Well, you have been very welcoming. You sent over a birthday cupcake and invited me to dance at a wedding where I only knew a few people."

She laughs, a cackling sort of laugh. "There is no welcoming committee. Skylar told me what a problem you were, and after I spoke to you for a bit, I realized you were exactly what she needs. You're grounded while she's floating around, doing her creative hippy thing." She flutters her hand in the air. "She's a golden beam of light, and you're a man who needs that in his life. The perfect yin and yang."

I swallow over the lump of emotion lodged in my throat. Skylar *is* golden. I knew that all along and came to appreciate it. I gather the food and napkins as Mrs. Ellis directs me to a nearby picnic table. Maybe since she saw the potential with me and Skylar, she'll also have the solution to my problem—how to get her back.

I take a seat across from her at the picnic table. She settles a paper napkin in her lap and takes a bite of hot dog.

I take a bite of burger, thinking about how best to state the problem. Skylar said Mrs. Ellis was her third-grade teacher, which means she must know Skylar well.

"She won't return my phone calls," I say.

"What did you do?"

I'm about to ask what makes her think it's my fault, but what's the point of placing blame?

"All I did was fix a major career problem for her. She told me she'd handle it herself, but her efforts were completely inadequate, so I stepped in. Now she's all set, problem solved, but she resents my help." *Isn't that what you're supposed to do when you love someone?*

"So you crossed the line of what's acceptable to her. Did you apologize sincerely?"

I swallow hard, my appetite vanishing. "She's the one who should be thanking me. I fixed what she couldn't fix."

She shakes her head and goes back to eating her lunch.

"That's it? No advice?" I grab my plate and napkin. "I'm going to go."

She grabs my wrist. "Sit down and wait for an old woman to finish her gosh-darn lunch. Geez, you young people, always in a hurry for the next thing."

There is no next thing. It's over.

God, when did I become this pathetic guy? This is what love does to you—wrings you out until you barely recognize yourself. The worst.

Excruciatingly slow moments later, after waiting for Mrs.

Ellis to eat a hot dog, pickle, and drink her water, she daintily wipes her mouth and finally says something useful to me.

"Skylar is special. You'll never find such a kind, big-hearted person full of joy in your life. She's been like this since she was a small child. Always looking at the world through the rosiest lens, giving generously, never holding anything back. Do you know when she was in my class, she made me handmade cards and paper cutouts that were quite extraordinarily detailed for a third grader. Flowers, hearts, snowflakes. Every occasion she made sure I had something, even though she was a little intimidated by me." She smiles widely, her eyes lighting up with the memory. "She'd race up, hand me her gift, and run away." She laughs. "If she'd stayed long enough, I could've thanked her, but I guess my rep for being strict preceded me."

"I know she's special. I've never met anyone like her."

She taught me how to open up to a person and have a real relationship. My throat closes, and I can't get the words out. It's too personal, anyway. I just stew in the fact that she gave me everything and then took it away.

Mrs. Ellis cocks her head, studying me for a moment, and then pats my hand. "I'm the one who gave Skylar the roses for Valentine's Day. I thought she would go to the guy she hoped they were from and ask if they were from him. I know for a fact she didn't rush straight to Levi. I checked."

"She went to me." She must've been hoping they were from me. And what did I do? Brush her off.

"Can I speak plainly?" she asks.

"Isn't that what you've been doing all along?"

She laughs her big, cackling laugh. "You look miserable without her. I did my part, and now it's your turn."

"She won't talk to me."

"Then you talk to her. Apologize and let her know how much you love her. It's that simple. She's not one to hold a grudge, and I think if you made even the *smallest* of efforts, she'd forgive you and take you back."

I rub the back of my neck. Could it really be that easy?

"But then I'd have to admit to wrongdoing when I did the right thing."

"It was only the right thing in your eyes. Isn't the way she feels about it what really matters? She felt strongly enough to end things with you over it."

All that matters is getting her back. I can still think I'm right and accept that Skylar doesn't agree. It's her feelings that matter here. It's her life, her career, her decisions. Even though it's really, really hard for me to stand by and do nothing, I shouldn't have gone behind her back. I see the problem clearly now.

"Thanks, Mrs. Ellis. I'll give it a try."

"Great!" She points over my shoulder. "The garden club is selling flowers. Go pick up some and take them to her little cottage at her brother's house."

"Is she at home?" She wasn't when I checked earlier.

"If she's not, you can just wait for her there. Nothing like a face-to-face conversation when love is on the line."

The word "love" sends adrenaline through me. I can't lose it when I just found it.

I stand and gather our trash. "If this works out, I'll do any renovation you want on your house for free."

She smiles. "My son-in-law, Garrett, can fix anything, so I'm all set. I'm just happy to help another couple find love. It's my thing. Ask around."

I don't see a strict general in front of me, all I see is a kindly old woman. I impulsively lean down and kiss her cheek. "I wish I had a grandmother like you in my life."

"Careful! I might adopt you into the family! They might start calling you colonel."

I grin. She's in on the General Joan thing. "It would be an honor."

She waves that away. "Go! Before someone else sweeps her off her feet."

I stiffen, but then I realize she's just trying to motivate me. I don't need motivation. I've got an urgency in me now that has me running over to the garden tent.

I arrive slightly out of breath and say to the cashier, "Hi, I'll take everything."

~

Skylar

I walk out the back door of Max and Brooke's house and head for the studio apartment in back, coming to a dead stop. Gage sits on the front step, surrounded by too many flowers to count in bouquets and a variety of pots. It looks like he bought out a flower store. There's daffodils, tulips, roses, irises, and some I don't know the name of. Actually, those pots and arrangements look like what the gardening club sells at the Spring Fling every year.

My lips curve up. "Did you buy the whole gardening club's inventory?"

"Yup."

"All for me? You know my brother's a landscaper. There's no shortage of plantings around here."

He stares at me.

"I mean thank you."

He pats the seat next to him. "C'mere."

I sit next to him.

"We should be together," he half growls.

My heart leaps. "Is that so?"

"Yes, and you know it. I'm sorry if I did something you didn't like, but you have to admit, it worked out."

"That's not an apology."

"All of this." He gestures around him to the flowers and then grabs a bouquet of tulips and shakes it. "This is my apology."

I take a deep breath. "I don't think you really get what the problem is. I can handle my life, and I don't want you taking over or going behind my back."

"But I fixed it!" He takes a deep breath. "No, wait, I get that you don't have to agree with me."

I sigh and stand. "Excuse me." I open my front door.

He stands and gestures to the door. "You should lock that."

"I was just next door."

"See how I look out for you? You need me."

I walk inside. "Bye, Gage."

"Dammit! Mrs. Ellis said this would work!"

"Mrs. Ellis?"

He gestures wildly. "Yes, with the flowers and the apologizing. Sky, those Valentine's Day roses you thought were from me, they were from Mrs. Ellis. She hoped you'd go to the guy you wanted them to be from, and I so wish I'd been the one to give them to you. It would've saved so much time and spared me this awful heart pain." He rubs his chest. "You're walking around out here with my heart, leaving me all vulnerable and achy. It's the worst kind of pain, you know?"

I rub his chest, touched by his openness. "I do know."

He places his hand over mine. "I love you. We belong together. And I'll never go behind your back again. From now on, if I want to fix your problems, I'll get you on board with the solution."

I wrap my arms around his neck. "Or I'll come up with my own solution."

"Agreed." He pushes a lock of hair behind my ear. "Does this mean…"

I kiss him softly. "I love you too with all my heart."

He presses his forehead to mine, his eyes shining with love. "Sky, I missed you so much."

"Show me."

And then I pull him inside to fully make up with him in private. With a guy like Gage, action is often much better than words. Though his words are fantastic too!

EPILOGUE

Two months later...

Gage

I count myself a lucky man. I found a woman who told me exactly how to show her love so she always knows how much I care. She loves words, and she figured out that I like small gestures. Only Skylar would take the guesswork out of a relationship. It's super easy to do too. I just added "love words" to my bullet list of things to do, right after taking care of Ace in the morning.

Sky moved back in with me, so I either think up some love words to leave on a note for her somewhere around the house, or on the weekends I get a little more creative and search the internet for song lyrics and bits of poetry that sound loving and write them on the whiteboard in her home office. So far she hasn't figured out I'm borrowing from the internet. Ha. All that matters is that she knows deep down how much I love her.

And you know what? She appreciates it so much she does lots of love things for me too. Little presents, notes, filling my truck with gas for me, baking cookies (the healthy kind, but what can you do?), or joining me in the shower to wash my hair and a few other primo spots. That's my favorite.

Today's the day I've been waiting for. I didn't tell Skylar where we were going, but of course she recognized the landmarks the moment we got close. We're back in Summerdale, her hometown. She didn't take the apartment she had lined up in favor of being with me. All this time she's been commuting back to clients here. I hope that will change for the better soon.

I take a turn onto Lakeshore Drive and pull into the driveway of a small cottage, one of the last original homes on Lake Summerdale. If Skylar's into this place, it's ours. If not, one day I'll build a lakeside home for her. That's what I do, find solutions to problems. Right now it's a problem that Skylar wants to live here in Summerdale and is living with me in New Jersey instead. Her family's here, and the lake is part of who she is. My only family is Livvie, and she's not too far away. I know she'll be okay with her fiancé. Charles is a good guy. They graduated last month and both got jobs at a hospital not far from their university. They plan to marry next year in June. She's happy, so I'm happy.

"Gage, what're we doing here?" Skylar asks, staring at the cottage. It resembles the place she grew up in with an addition on the side.

"This is the place Spencer used to rent. It's owned by an older couple who spent a lot of time in Virginia to be near their grandkids."

"Mr. and Mrs. Fisher, I know."

"They want to sell. Spencer told me about it before they put it on the market, so I was thinking, how about I sell my house and we get this lake house like you always dreamed of? We could renovate this place or start fresh with something new I build to your specifications. Whatever you want."

She grabs my arm in a tight grip. "Are you serious? I never thought I'd get to live on the lake again. You sure you wouldn't mind moving so far from Livvie?"

"She's not that far away for visits. Besides, she's a grown woman who doesn't need me to help raise her anymore. She's got this."

She kisses me. "So wise. Can we go inside?"

"Yup. I have the key."

I get out of the truck and meet her on the other side, taking her hand. "But first, let's take in the view of the lake."

We walk over to the shoreline. It's a beautiful warm June day, the leaves in their full greenery. A family of baby ducks swim by with their mother.

"Oh, how cute!" she exclaims, smiling at them.

I take the ring from my pocket and go down on one knee.

She takes in the lake view. "It's the opposite side of the lake from where I grew up, so it's a new perspective, yet still my favorite spot in the world." She turns to me and gasps, her hand flying to her mouth.

"Sky, you've taught me so much about love and true intimacy, opening my heart in ways I didn't think were possible."

Her eyes well, and my own eyes sting. I swallow over the now familiar lump of emotion lodged in my throat. Only Skylar can bring out these deep feelings with one look. "I thought I was rescuing you by taking you in and giving you a job and fighting your battles for you, but really it was you who rescued me and brought joy into my life. I even shake things up now and then, like now. This house wasn't even on my bullet list, but I heard about it and leaped at the chance."

"Oh, Gage."

"I love you with all my heart, and I'll love you for the rest of my life. Will you marry me?"

"Yes!"

I put the ring on her finger, my hand a little unsteady. I'm overwhelmed by all I'm feeling, in a good way.

I stand and fold her into my arms, where she fits perfectly.

She hugs me tight and looks up at me. "I loved all your love words in that proposal. You didn't rip them off from a song or poem, did you? Those were Gage originals, right?"

Damn, she was onto me before.

I kiss her. "That proposal was a Gage original. You have changed me for the better, you know."

She smiles widely. "I know. And you changed me for the better too. All your slow and steady decision-making has made me slow down and not be so impulsive. And just to prove it, I'm going to contribute toward our house with money I've saved. See how I thought ahead to the future by saving money?"

"See how I shook things up? I'm moving for you."

"Oh, it's not so bad here. Mrs. Ellis adores you, you're close with Spencer, and I bet you'll have new clients in no time."

"True. Brooke and I are teaming up. She snags architecture clients, and I come in with the renovation or construction work. We'll recommend you for interior design and mural work naturally."

"Perfect! Now let's go check out our new house."

I pull the key from my pocket and go to the front door. "Wait, how did you know I already bought it?"

"Because you wouldn't risk showing me a place you couldn't deliver on. I know your word is a rock-solid promise."

"Damn, you're going to be hard to surprise."

"That's right," she says smugly. "I know you inside and out."

I open the door and let her go in first. The lights flash on, and our family and friends shout, "Surprise!"

Skylar shrieks and whirls, burying her head in my chest.

I stroke her head, chuckling. "You okay?"

"Did *not* expect that. I think they scared ten years off my life."

I tip her chin up and kiss her. "You'll survive. Let's go in. It's our first cookout at our new place."

Spencer congratulates us and goes outside to get his grill started. Her brothers rush us first to congratulate us. I glance around as Skylar exclaims over her surprise to her brothers and how sneaky they were. They clearly adore her, looking enthralled with her bubbly enthusiasm.

A lot of couples from town are gathered around a few card tables full of appetizers Spencer prepared. I'm about to make the rounds, thanking everyone for coming, when Mrs. Ellis appears in front of us.

"So good to see you here, Cupid!" Skylar exclaims.

They laugh. Mrs. Ellis gestures toward the crowd and announces, "I take full credit for every couple here."

Laughter and low conversation breaks out among the supposed couples she brought together.

"Guess who's next?" Skylar asks, pointing to Mrs. Ellis, but Mrs. Ellis doesn't notice. Her eyes are on Levi.

"You're right. It's his turn. No doubt about it. Now where's Audrey?"

Just then Audrey rushes in from the kitchen, her face flushed pink, followed by a shocked-looking Drew. "I'm right here!"

∽

Skylar

After everyone goes home, Gage and I sit in the living room of our new house, talking about plans for it. He agrees with everything I say design-wise, which immediately makes me suspicious.

"You never have no opinion. Stop being so agreeable and tell me what you think."

"I'm thinking I really need to take you to bed."

"What bed?"

He scoops me up and carries me to the larger of the two bedrooms. I gasp. There's twinkle lights hanging from the ceiling around a sheer canopy over a bed covered with a fluffy blanket and many pillows. It reminds me of a harem scene, except I'm the only woman here.

"When did you do this?" I ask, truly surprised.

"After your tour. Remember when Mrs. Ellis asked you to drive her home? That was so I could do setup."

"No wonder she kept piling on the requests! She made me drive to pick up something at the pharmacy, something at The Horseman Inn, and Summerdale Sweets. She said those last two were because her granddaughter, Harper, was visiting soon with her family."

"Nice and vague that 'soon.'"

"I should've known something was up. Crafty lady. And crafty you." I rub his chest.

He sets me on my feet, banding an arm around my waist to keep me pressed close against him. "Enough talk," he growls before his mouth crashes down over mine. A rush of dizzying lust hits me, and I melt against him.

Long moments later, he parts the sheer drapery, and I crawl onto the soft mattress. "This is amazing. We should always sleep like this."

"I don't plan on getting much sleep."

I rip off his clothes as he rips off mine. He pauses for the condom, and then he's on me, his mouth claiming mine just as his body does. It's hot, urgent, primal. A fiery joining that steals my breath. *More, more, more.* I can't get close enough, my arms and legs wrapped around him as he drives into me. The orgasm takes me by surprise in a shuddering fall that leaves us both gasping in the aftermath.

He strokes my hair back from my face. "I love you, Skylar Bellamy. You are my world. The smartest, most beautiful, creative woman I've ever met."

He's so good with the love words!

"I love you with all my heart, and I can't wait for a future with you. I'm going to make you a special present." He likes tokens of affection to know he's loved, or sometimes just a small gesture. We read a book about love languages to be sure we each felt loved deeply. It was my idea, but he was on board right away.

He smiles, lighting up his gorgeous face. "Because you love me so much."

"Yes."

"Is it a baby?"

"Are you serious?"

He strokes my hair back. "I'd love a little Skylar or two running around here."

"What about a little Gage?"

"Oh, I don't know, he'd be a handful. Headstrong and stubborn."

"A true leader, and a man of his word."

He kisses me. "So kids?"

"Yes, but let's wait for a little while, spend some time just us while we get our new home ready, and don't forget our huge wedding with all the fixings."

He suppresses a wince. "Whatever you want."

"I'd like to get married at the lake."

"Outdoor wedding. Cool."

"And invite the whole town."

"The whole town," he echoes.

"Everyone."

"Cool."

"Awesome!"

He looks into my eyes intently. "That's a lot of people."

"Haven't you noticed how much this town likes a festival? This will be our wedding festival."

"Okay, you make it exactly the way you like it, and I'll, uh, show up."

"Oh no, we both have to come up with it so we're both happy."

"You're the creative one. It's all you, Sky."

"How about you build a dock where we can have the ceremony?"

"Done."

I play with the hair at the nape of his neck, and he closes his eyes, enjoying my touch. "But kids and planning the wedding event of the century aren't my only gift for you."

"Yeah?" he murmurs. "What is it?"

"You'll see."

His eyes fly open in alarm.

$\sim$

And there it hangs right in our front hallway. I painted the lake and our cottage and framed it as my engagement gift to him.

"Gorgeous!" he exclaims. "Be right back."

Then he surprises me, putting a Post-it on the corner of the frame that's in my writing: *Does not work well with others. Flaw #734.*

So sweet that he saved that!

He puts an arm around me. "That's the day I realized you were into me. You couldn't stop thinking about me and all my flaws, so I knew there had to be something between us."

I sigh. "You were right. And now look how well we work together."

"I'm always right."

I shoot him a look.

"Except when I'm not."

We walk outside, hand in hand, to admire the sunset on our new dock. Everything I've ever wanted is right here—my beloved lake, my beloved, and a future filled with love.

Don't miss the next book in the series, *Leading*, where Mayor Levi finds himself on a honeymoon in Vegas with a jilted bride!

A jilted bride, a swoony wedding officiant, and a honeymoon trip to Vegas that shouldn't go to waste...

Galena

You know what's worse than being a jilted bride? Getting a text from the groom that he's not coming while a magazine is there to cover the event. Shock doesn't begin to describe my reaction or my impulsive next move. I'm a biostatistician, which means I'm quick to calculate the odds, and I was so sure of him after our two-year relationship. If I could be wrong about him, then my careful calculations no longer apply to my life.

So when the gorgeous wedding officiant, Mayor Levi Appleton, comes to my rescue, whisking me away on a thrilling ride on his Harley, I impulsively invite him to join me on my honeymoon in Vegas. It's paid for, and my grandparents are expecting to meet my new husband for the first time. And he agrees to go! I would never have calculated that outcome.

I don't want to disappoint my grandparents, so I let them believe Levi is my forever love. And they love him.

What are the odds I'd fall for him too? Tiny. So tiny it's ridiculous. Can this possibly be real?

Sign up for my newsletter and never miss a new release! kyliegilmore.com/newsletter

ALSO BY KYLIE GILMORE

Unleashed Romance <<steamy romcoms with dogs!

Fetching (Book 1)

Dashing (Book 2)

Sporting (Book 3)

Toying (Book 4)

Blazing (Book 5)

Chasing (Book 6)

Daring (Book 7)

Leading (Book 8)

Racing (Book 9)

Loving (Book 10)

The Clover Park Series <<brothers who put family first!

The Opposite of Wild (Book 1)

Daisy Does It All (Book 2)

Bad Taste in Men (Book 3)

Kissing Santa (Book 4)

Restless Harmony (Book 5)

Not My Romeo (Book 6)

Rev Me Up (Book 7)

An Ambitious Engagement (Book 8)

Clutch Player (Book 9)

A Tempting Friendship (Book 10)

Clover Park Bride: Nico and Lily's Wedding

A Valentine's Day Gift (Book 11)

Maggie Meets Her Match (Book 12)

The Clover Park STUDS series <<hawt geeks who unleash into studs!

Almost Over It (Book 1)

Almost Married (Book 2)

Almost Fate (Book 3)

Almost in Love (Book 4)

Almost Romance (Book 5)

Almost Hitched (Book 6)

Happy Endings Book Club Series <<the Campbell family and a romance book club collide!

Hidden Hollywood (Book 1)

Inviting Trouble (Book 2)

So Revealing (Book 3)

Formal Arrangement (Book 4)

Bad Boy Done Wrong (Book 5)

Mess With Me (Book 6)

Resisting Fate (Book 7)

Chance of Romance (Book 8)

Wicked Flirt (Book 9)

An Inconvenient Plan (Book 10)

A Happy Endings Wedding (Book 11)

The Rourkes Series <<swoonworthy princes and kickass princesses!

Royal Catch (Book 1)

Royal Hottie (Book 2)

Royal Darling (Book 3)

Royal Charmer (Book 4)

Royal Player (Book 5)

Royal Shark (Book 6)

Rogue Prince (Book 7)

Rogue Gentleman (Book 8)

**Check out my website for the most up-to-date list of my books:
kyliegilmore.com/books**

ABOUT THE AUTHOR

Kylie Gilmore is the *USA Today* bestselling author of the Unleashed Romance series, the Rourkes series, the Happy Endings Book Club series, the Clover Park series, and the Clover Park STUDS series. She writes humorous romance that makes you laugh, cry, and reach for a cold glass of water.

Kylie lives in New York with her family, two cats, and a nutso dog. When she's not writing, reading hot romance, or dutifully taking notes at writing conferences, you can find her flexing her muscles all the way to the high cabinet for her secret chocolate stash.

Sign up for Kylie's Newsletter and get a FREE book! kyliegilmore.com/newsletter

For text alerts on Kylie's new releases, text KYLIE to the number (888) 707-3025. (US only)

For more fun stuff check out Kylie's website https://www.kyliegilmore.com.

Thanks for reading *Daring*. I hope you enjoyed it. Would you like to know about new releases? You can sign up for my new release email list at kyliegilmore.com/newsletter. I promise not to clog your inbox! Only new release info, sales, and some fun giveaways.

I love to hear from readers! You can find me at:
kyliegilmore.com
Instagram.com/kyliegilmore
Facebook.com/KylieGilmoreToo
Twitter @KylieGilmoreToo

If you liked Gage and Skylar's story, please leave a review on your favorite retailer's website or Goodreads. Thank you.

Manufactured by Amazon.ca
Bolton, ON

24970547R00120